09328509

SPECIAL MESSA...

T... ...t

TH... ...N

J...

resea... ...ses.

DI 4/13

CR → LE

AT 11/14

Roy... ...ts.

CV 7/15

T...

Great 12/4/22 ...ren,

You ... ...tion
by n... ...ery
con... ...ed

w...

TH... ...I,

GW00775847

TH... ...
c/o The Royal Australi...
College of Ophthalmologists,
94-98 Chalmers Street, Surry Hills,
N.S.W. 2010, Australia

DEAD ON TIME

When Jonathan Boot, the Mayor of Mallerton District Council, dies a very public and bizarre death, in the middle of a council meeting, Inspector Cobb's investigation leads him into a world of suspicion, adultery and deceit. Convinced that the mayor's unexplained wealth is the key to solving the crime, Cobb must decide where a missing art collection, the biggest surprise in horse-racing history and allegations of bribery fit into his inquiries. Then as two further murders occur, Cobb fears a fourth victim may be lined up. He knows who the potential victim might be — although he doesn't know why . . .

Books by Veronyca Bates
Published by The House of Ulverscroft:

DEAD IN THE WATER

VERONYCA BATES

DEAD ON TIME

Complete and Unabridged

ULVERSCROFT
Leicester

First published in Great Britain in 2011 by
Robert Hale Limited
London

First Large Print Edition
published 2012
by arrangement with
Robert Hale Limited
London

British Library CIP Data

Bates, Veronyca.
  Dead on time.
  1. Murder- -Investigation- -England- -Fiction.
  2. Police- -England- -Fiction.
  3. Detective and mystery stories.
  4. Large type books.
  I. Title
  823.9'2–dc23

  ISBN 978–1–4448–1170–4

Published by
F. A. Thorpe (Publishing)
Anstey, Leicestershire

Set by Words & Graphics Ltd.
Anstey, Leicestershire
Printed and bound in Great Britain by
T. J. International Ltd., Padstow, Cornwall

This book is printed on acid-free paper

1

'Mr Mayor, if you please. I have a question to ask.' Quentin Makepeace bobbed up and down in agitation, his hand windmilling above his head.

The mayor, Councillor Jonathan Boot, took his time. Although he dropped his gaze to the papers before him, he wasn't quick enough, and all present in the council chamber saw the disdainful, almost sneering look on his face. When he spoke his words were tinged with what might well be called sarcasm. 'Mr Makepeace, I shall allow you to ask your question. You have three minutes.' He started the clock but set it for only two and a half minutes. Democracy had its limits, after all, and if Jonathan Boot had his way the public would not have the opportunity to question what he got up to; especially someone like Quentin Makepeace who was enjoying himself just a shade too much. The public gallery was packed, as was the modern, amphitheatre-style council chamber with all sixty-two councillors crammed onto the benches.

Amphitheatre was a good word for the

chamber. Many a battle had been fought here and blood spilt — metaphorically, that is — on more than one occasion. Pity it wasn't for real, in several cases, Boot mused.

Quentin droned on, but the mayor had stopped listening. He felt as if someone had turned a flamethrower on him. If only he hadn't had to open a community centre that morning, he'd have had time for a proper lunch before chairing this wretched council meeting. As it was, lack of time meant he couldn't go out to a decent restaurant but had to make do with the council offices canteen, and there had been nothing left but curry or a vegetable Kiev — whatever that was — so he took the curry as the lesser of two evils. Whether it was the curry that was making him feel so strange, or the dire refreshments the community centre committee had laid on as part of the celebrations, he didn't know, but something must have been off.

Food poisoning, that was just marvellous. And he wouldn't be able to sue either. As mayor that just wouldn't be right. He'd bloody well complain though. Someone would get a kick up the backside for this.

Water. He needed water desperately. Preferably a fire engine's worth to douse the heat that was consuming him. There was a jug of water and some glasses on the bench in front of him, but his sight was suddenly blurry. He could hardly see a thing and he groped frantically around, his hand flapping convulsively like a dying fish.

Everyone could see something was very wrong indeed with the mayor. Quentin stopped in mid tirade to ask, 'Are you all right, Mr Mayor?'

'Yes, yes, carry on,' Jonathan said weakly, mopping his brow with a handkerchief.

'Are you sure you're all right?' John Wilson, the monitoring officer seated to the right of the mayor, leant over and whispered in Jonathan's ear. 'You look very flushed and hot.'

In reply, the mayor hauled himself to his feet and with a shaking hand pointed to the back of the room. 'What's that zebra doing in here? Call security and tell them to remove it immediately!' he shrieked, and started clawing at his clothes. 'Help me, someone. For pity's sake, get these spiders off me!' His voice rose to an incomprehensible gibber, then he staggered and with a crash toppled over the bench just as the buzzer went off to let Quentin Makepeace know his time was up.

★ ★ ★

DI Steve Cobb squeezed his car into the last space in the car park at the back of the police station and turned both the wipers and the heating off. It was the first Monday in July and he could only assume whoever had named it 'global warming' had a wry sense of humour.

As he hurried across the open space, collar turned up against the wind and the rain, he saw the tall figure of his sergeant ahead.

'Hey, Neil. Just a moment,' he called into the wind.

Neil Bould turned round. 'Good morning, sir. How are you?'

'There's nothing good about this morning,' his boss grumbled in reply. That was the trouble with young love — it put the recipient in such a damned good mood all the time. Ever since Bould had got engaged to PC Cathy Treharris he'd been like this. 'Come to my office in ten minutes. We need to talk through a problem.'

'Is it going to be a one-doughnut problem or a two-doughnut problem?'

'Whilst I am flattered to be compared to Sherlock Holmes, there's going to be no bloody doughnuts for the moment,' Cobb replied as he keyed his security code into the door lock. Bould had hit a nerve there. At his annual medical last week the doctor had found his cholesterol level was still higher than it should be. Foolishly, he told his wife Sarah and now he was back on a diet of steamed fish and broccoli. Doughnuts were out for the time being.

When Bould put his head round the DI's door a bit later, he found Cobb engrossed in the contents of a slim manilla file.

Looking up, Cobb said, 'Come in, Sergeant. Tell me, what do you know about Jonathan Boot?'

It took a moment or two for the connection to be made. 'The mayor of Mallerton District Council who died during a council meeting last week? Nothing, other than what I read in the paper the day after it happened. Do I take it there's something untoward about his death?'

'You do indeed. Seems he was murdered.' Cobb went over to the coffee percolator permanently on the boil and poured himself a cup, then waved the jug in Bould's direction, who nodded his acceptance. Cobb poured a second cup and brought both back to the desk. This was the time when he really wanted a doughnut to chew on and his mood darkened. 'I read about his death too and it seems the public thought the world of him, if the local press is to be believed. You'd think the man was a positive saint from the gnashing of teeth and renting of clothes going on.'

'Someone couldn't have liked him very much though,' Bould observed, taking a seat.

'No indeed. It's perverse the way people say of a murder victim 'he hadn't an enemy in the world' when they're staring at the dead body . . . It was atropine that killed him, according to Bolton.'

Dr Samuel Bolton was their new pathologist. He had taken over from Jenny Sutherland, newly retired and much missed. Cobb tried to tell himself it was early days and he might yet get to like Bolton, but somehow he doubted it. The man was arrogant and offhand.

'Atropine? That's a very unusual poison,' Bould observed, taking the post mortem report handed to him.

'Isn't it just. It's mostly used by doctors in resuscitation and also for certain eye conditions apparently, and it's also an antidote for another poison, strangely, but there's no doubt about it, according to Bolton. Not that he's had the toxicology report back yet and we'll need that to confirm it, but apparently Boot displayed all the classic symptoms.' At this point he consulted the pathologist's notes and read aloud: 'Hot as a hare, blind as a bat, dry as a bone, red as a beet and mad as a hatter.'

'Sir?' Bould was too circumspect to say anything more, although he raised an eyebrow.

'That's what it says here. Bolton tells me that's what medical students are taught as a means of recognizing atropine poisoning. It's quite specific, I think you'll agree.'

'So we're looking for someone with a medical background. That should narrow the field considerably,' Bould said as he speed read the report.

'Not necessarily. Atropine is what makes deadly nightshade deadly,' his boss replied with some gloom. 'So it could be anyone who knows that and also knows a spot where the stuff grows.'

'Is it common these days? I remember seeing it in hedgerows when I was a boy but I can't say I've seen it at all lately — and how do you extract the poison from the plant, anyway?'

Cobb shrugged, the answers beyond him. 'No doubt a herbalist would know, so we might have to find one to tell us. On the other hand, it might not be relevant. You could be right; it could be a doctor we're looking for. We'll start with basics.' He stood up. 'Let's go and talk to the widow — see what she has to say.'

Cobb peered through the rivulets of rain cascading down the windscreen. 'Foinavon.' He read aloud the name of the late mayor's residence from a large brass plate attached to one of a pair of impressive stone pillars, topped with ornamental griffins. 'So Boot was a racing man.'

'Not the most obvious horse to be drawn to,' Bould said as the car crunched its way up a wide sweep of a gravel drive towards the large detached neo-classical-style house.

They were received by a slim young man who introduced himself as Adam Boot.

'My mother will be down shortly. She's just sorting out Father's things,' he told the officers as he showed them into what Cobb thought of as a drawing room.

'Some money here,' Cobb muttered once the son had withdrawn. He prowled around the room, taking in the expensive antiques, heavy curtains and deep pile carpet.

Bould moved over to the French windows and looked out at the immaculate lawn. 'Where did the money come from for all this? According to the paper Boot made a virtue of being a man of the people.'

'Looks like that didn't extend to living like one of them as well.'

'Ah, Inspector Cobb, sorry I wasn't here to meet you.' Sylvia Boot, dry eyed and looking more businesslike than bereaved, had entered the room silently. If she had heard the last exchange she didn't show it.

'Good morning, Mrs Boot. We've very sorry to have to trouble you at such a time, and we'll try to keep it as short as possible, but there are some questions we need to ask.'

'Of course. Please do sit down.' With a sweep of her hand she indicated the assortment of furniture available. A chaise longue upholstered in dusky pink velvet, a bow-legged ormolu chair in the same fabric, or one of a pair of comfortable wing chairs in dusky blue. The gracious tone of her voice suggested she was doing them a huge favour in granting this audience.

The officers waited until their hostess had seated herself and then Cobb claimed the bow-legged chair and Bould settled for one of the winged pair.

'As you probably realize, we're investigating your husband's death. Are you aware of any threats made against him? Is there anyone who might have had a grudge that you know of?' Cobb cut straight to the chase as Bould got his notebook out.

Sylvia Boot shook her immaculately coiffured silver head. 'Absolutely not. Jonathan was simply adored by everyone who knew him.'

Cobb kept his thoughts on that one to himself. 'So he had no enemies that you are aware of?'

'He had no enemies; of that I am sure.'

With many bereaved people, Cobb knew this sentiment was purely down to denial but with Mrs Boot he had a feeling it was pure intransigence. 'Are you sure you can think of no one who would wish your husband harm? Someone he might have crossed? In his role as a councillor could he have made any political enemies?'

'Well, I really wouldn't know about that side of his life. Politics doesn't interest me at all, and if that's all you wanted to ask me I'm afraid I'm not going to be able to help you at all.' With a fixed smile she rose to her feet, clearly indicating the audience was over, but just in case they didn't get the message she added: 'I'm sorry, but this really isn't a very good time. Perhaps you could telephone to make an appointment if you need to speak to me again.'

'Madam, we're investigating your husband's murder, not offering a hairdressing service.' Cobb was almost apoplectic. If he had believed she was finding the interview distressing he would have been more than sympathetic, but he didn't. In fact he was of the opinion he was in the company of a brisk and uncaring woman.

Realizing she had gone too far, Sylvia raised a white hand to her forehead and spoke distantly, almost as if she might be on the point of fainting. 'No, of course not. I do understand, but I don't feel quite myself at the moment. I do hope you can excuse me.'

Mollified somewhat at having brought her to heel, Cobb went on. 'Your husband was a surveyor, I believe.'

'That is right. He was the senior partner in Swallow & Carrick. They have always been such a successful firm, but I fear with Jonathan gone poor Peter Smith will find it very hard.' There was a snide undertone to her faux sympathy for 'poor Peter Smith'.

'And why is that?' Cobb asked.

Sylvia made a small movement with her hands. 'If you'd ever met my husband, Mr Cobb, you'd know just what a great character he was. A lot of Swallow & Carrick's clients were only with them because of Jonathan. I doubt they'll stay with Peter — who is a very conscientious man but totally lacks the . . . *je ne sais quoi.*' She finished with a rather self-deprecating smile and gazed sadly at the officers.

'We'll also need to speak to his solicitor

— can you supply us with his name?'

'What for?' There was a hard edge to her voice and her eyes became narrow slits. All sense of graciousness had vanished.

'Mrs Boot, someone has killed your husband. We need to find out why.' Cobb was patient, as if spelling it out for a child.

'Well, David Bartley won't know.'

'David Bartley. Thank you very much, madam. I think that's all for the time being.'

'You don't come from round here?' Bould said conversationally as they waited for her to open the front door and see them out.

Turning, she smiled thinly, clearly not thanking him for the unspoken inference that she had an accent. 'No indeed. That's very perspicacious of you. I come from London originally.'

'So was it marriage that brought you here?'

'It was. I met Jonathan in London when we were students in the seventies. It was love at first sight.'

Cobb couldn't help but think that it hadn't lasted then, as she appeared so little upset at her husband's death. 'Just one last thing, Mrs Boot. Do you mind if we take a look at your garden?'

The request baffled her. They could see it on her face. 'Why?'

'We're looking for deadly nightshade.'

'I don't think you'll find anything like that here, but be my guests.'

★ ★ ★

Sylvia remained on the step, watching Bould and Cobb until they vanished from sight round the house, as if she wanted to make sure checking the garden was all they were going to do. Once they disappeared from her view, she started to turn away but the sight of the postman marching up the drive stopped her dead in her tracks. He had only one envelope in his hand — a cream deckle, quite distinctive — but it was enough to freeze her to the spot.

'Morning, Mrs B. Just this for you today.' His voice, habitually cheery, was the same as ever. Of course it was; he had no idea there was a ticking bomb inside the innocent-looking missive he carried.

Did her hand tremble as she took it? Probably, but he would assume she was still grief stricken and think nothing of it.

No need to look at the handwriting for confirmation, but her eyes were drawn to it compulsively. Her name and address written in neat capital letters in black ink — ridiculously the thought crossed her mind that it was so nice to see some people still used a proper fountain pen to write with — confirmed what she had been dreading.

Moving quickly, she headed for the safety of her bedroom. Adam must never know about these letters. She had thought — hoped — they would stop now that Jonathan was dead. After all, wasn't that what the sender had wanted — her husband's death?

2

Bould swung the car into the shoebox that passed for Swallow & Carrick's car park and pulled up in front of the modest entrance. 'Hardly looks the sort of place his wife led us to believe,' he observed.

Overnight the weather had played one of its peculiarly British tricks and changed. Summer had now come in with a vengeance, as if deciding to make up for lost time, and the temperature had risen by a good ten degrees. Squinting into the bright sunlight that had replaced the rain, Cobb looked up at the façade. 'The building could certainly do with some maintenance right enough. Come on.' He pushed through the glass doors into a small reception area.

'Good morning, can I help you?' A young woman with a mass of curly blonde hair beamed happily at them.

Producing their warrant cards, the DI said: 'Mr Smith is expecting us.'

'Oh yes, he did say but unfortunately he's had to pop out for a moment. He said it was urgent but he'd only be about ten minutes. You can sit down if you like.' She waved them towards a couple of well-worn chairs leaning against the far wall.

Neither of the officers moved.

'We seem to be having a rare time of people not wanting to talk to us at the moment,' Cobb muttered to his sergeant. Raising his voice he addressed the receptionist. 'Thank you. Have you worked here long, Miss . . . '

'Amy Baker. Pleased to meet you, I'm sure. I've been here three months now.'

Such a short time. What a shame. It meant she would be very unlikely to have anything of use to tell them.

'Then you wouldn't have known Mr Boot very well.'

'No, I hardly saw him at all. He was very busy with his official duties,' she replied, putting great emphasis on the last two words.

'As mayor, you mean?' Bould asked for the sake of clarity.

She turned to him and nodded eagerly. 'That's right. He was a very important person in this town, you know.'

'Does that mean Mr Smith had to deal with all Mr Boot's clients as well as his own?'

'Yes, and I don't think he was very pleased about it. One day last week Mr Boot came in and they had a terrible row. You could hear them all over the building.'

16

'Did you hear what it was about?' Cobb asked.

'I'm so sorry to have kept you waiting.' A timid-looking, middle-aged man wearing a crumpled brown suit had entered quietly behind them. Holding out his hand, he introduced himself. 'Peter Smith. I do apologize for not being here when you arrived, but I see Amy has been looking after you. Shall we go into my office?'

Smith's office was upstairs and shabbier than the reception area. As soon as the door closed he said 'How can I help you?' in an agitated voice. He seemed jumpy and kept glancing towards the window.

'As you know we're investigating the death of your partner, Jonathan Boot,' Cobb began. 'At the moment we're simply making routine enquiries. Are you aware of any problems Mr Boot might have been having — anybody who might have a grudge against him, for example?'

'No, none. Nothing. Everyone liked Jonathan.'

'We've heard that you and he were arguing the other day.'

Smith's mouth opened and closed, then opened again. 'Who told you — ' he started, then worked it out for himself. His eyes fled to the window. He looked extremely unhappy.

Cobb waited.

With an effort, the surveyor pulled himself together, but addressed the window. 'Oh, yes, now I remember. It was nothing, just some triviality. I was hoping Jonathan could go and see a new client regarding a survey on a factory he was hoping to purchase. We do mostly commercial surveying here. Anyhow, Jonathan, being mayor this year, had little time for his professional duties and he hadn't been to do the job. The client was far from happy and I wouldn't really say it was a row we had, but I did let him know I was disappointed he wasn't able to have the input into the company he should at present.'

'I see. Is Swallow & Carrick doing well at the moment?'

'Yes, yes. We're doing better than ever.'

'I only ask because in the current economic climate a lot of small firms are struggling . . . ' Cobb let the rest of the sentence hang unfinished between them. There was certainly nothing about the way the office was furnished to encourage anyone to think Swallow & Carrick was doing well.

A forced smile. 'I can't say how others are doing, but we've no shortage of clients. Business is very satisfactory.'

'Will you continue alone or look for a new partner?' Bould enquired. He moved to the window to see just what it was that was

18

distracting Smith. There was nothing but a dusty alleyway and the blank wall of another Victorian semi-detached townhouse that had once been a family home, like the Swallow & Carrick building, but now housed a local charity.

'Good Lord, I haven't got as far as thinking about that yet. Jonathan's only been dead less than a week.' Then he demonstrated that he had been thinking about it. 'I'll probably carry on by myself. We've got a couple of employees who are qualified surveyors but I don't think I need another partner. It all depends.'

'On what?' Cobb said.

Smith looked baffled, and then frightened. He began blustering. 'Well, you know, various things.'

'No, I don't know. I'm a policeman — I've never really understood the mysteries of partnerships.' It wasn't true, of course, but Cobb had long since discovered playing the innocent often lulled the unwary into giving away more than they intended.

It seemed to work because Smith began explaining things. 'There's a great deal to be said for being a sole practitioner. The thing about partners is you really need an odd number so that if there is a difference of opinion you can get a majority vote in favour of one thing or another. With two, unless you both agree on everything, there can be problems.' Smith seemed pleased to be able to give the officers a little lecture on how the system worked and was blissfully unaware of how much information about his relationship with the late senior partner of Swallow & Carrick he had just given away.

3

'These are supposed to be the finest Victorian gardens in England; that's why they got ten million pounds from the Lottery to restore them,' Bould informed his boss, unfurling his body from the driver's seat.

'Ten million pounds!' The DI was scandalized. 'How can you spend ten million restoring a garden? What do they use for compost — gold dust?' He studied the near-deserted car park. 'It doesn't seem to have brought the crowds flocking for all that.'

'It is mid morning on a weekday, and the schools haven't broken up yet. Mr Boot told me that at the weekends and holidays it's packed. Apparently they're parking halfway to Gloucester.'

They hadn't gone to Latham to admire the gardens, but to interview Jonathan Boot's brother, William, who worked there.

'What makes a Victorian garden different to any other type? I can only see grass and trees from where I'm standing, and I can see those anywhere.' Cobb tilted his head skywards and gazed at a grand Georgian limestone façade. 'The house is impressive enough, I'll grant you that, though how a council can afford to purchase something like this is beyond me and I'm not even going to wonder *why* they would do it.'

They started to walk around the side of Latham Hall, gravel crunching beneath their feet. As the back of the house came into view the full glory of the gardens was revealed. Along the balustrade surrounding a long terrace a rampant wisteria grew. Beneath the terrace a lawn of almost infinite proportions swept away to a circular fountain. Water cascaded from the mouth of Neptune, triumphantly astride four plunging and bucketing horses. Beneath the terrace, and down the two long sides of the lawn, flower beds bursting with colour blazed.

'Glad to see the ten million has been put to good use,' Cobb said laconically, still wondering whether the money couldn't have been used better.

At the far end of the terrace they came across a modern annexe with the words 'Schools Centre' titled over the doorway.

The centre was deserted apart from a man in late middle age standing behind a counter and studying a brochure. He had a grey goatee beard and wore a black polo-neck sweater and black jeans.

'The last of the beatniks,' Cobb muttered

as they approached, then louder: 'Would you be Mr William Boot?'

'Indeed I would. And would you be Detective Inspector Cobb?'

'That's me, and this is Sergeant Bould. We'd like to talk to you about your brother.'

'Ah yes. Poor Jonathan. Such an extraordinary thing to happen.' William put down his brochure with a sigh.

'You work here, I understand?' Cobb started the interview.

'Yes, I'm in charge of restoration work in the house. We're hoping to get grants from various sources and eventually open it to the public as well. It's got some fine Adams interiors.'

'It strikes me the property would be better off in the hands of the National Trust rather than the council. I'd have thought this was totally outside their remit. Don't your residents prefer you to deal with more mundane matters like traffic and rubbish collections than acquiring country houses?' Cobb's tone was acerbic.

William regarded the DI curiously. 'So you don't know the story behind Latham Hall?'

'Clearly not.'

Nodding towards the door, William said: 'Why don't we take a turn about the gardens whilst I tell you? I find them tranquil and uplifting in the extreme.'

'So they should be for ten million pounds.'

They crossed the terrace, descended a shallow set of stone steps, turned through an archway and found themselves in ancient Rome.

'Good God,' Cobb said, taken aback.

A chuckle escaped William's lips. 'Fantastic, isn't it?'

'I thought it was supposed to be Victorian,' Bould said, equally surprised at the beautifully constructed Roman villa before them. Shady colonnades ran round three sides of the space with a fountain in the centre. This was a very modest affair compared to the one at the end of the main lawn. Water trickled out of a central spout and fell in a curtain over a circular disc. The sound was like that of a mountain stream.

'This side of the garden is a succession of rooms. Richard Latham, like many affluent Victorians, did the Grand Tour. When he came home he recreated the countries he had visited in his garden rooms.'

'Must have cost him a fortune,' Bould said.

'The Lathams had a fortune — once. They made their money out of shipping and woollen mills.'

Sensing that they were getting to the heart of the tale, Cobb asked: 'What happened to it?'

'When Alfred Latham died in 1984, his son Henry was faced with punitive death duties. He didn't want to sell the house and so came to an arrangement with the Inland Revenue in the way many of these families do. The Lathams had a famous art collection built up over many generations. There were a couple of Van Dykes, a Gainsborough or two, some Reynolds, and the Latham of his day was one of the first to recognize the potential of the Impressionists and Pre-Raphaelites. The collection was worth a great deal of money and so the Revenue agreed to take a couple of paintings in lieu of death duties — a Reynolds and a small piece by Degas, if I recall correctly.' William paused for dramatic effect and regarded Cobb out of the corner of his eye.

'So what went wrong?'

A thin smile of satisfaction creased William's lips. 'I'm glad you follow me, Inspector. What went wrong was that the paintings turned out not to be the originals.'

'You mean they were forgeries?' Bould interjected, ducking his head as they passed between colonnades thick with vines.

'Indeed they were, as every other painting in the collection turned out to be as well. The whole lot was worthless. Faced with financial ruin, as well as public humiliation, Henry shot himself. His son, faced with a further set of death duties and having no other means of raising the money, handed the house over to the government — which for practical purposes meant the council had to manage it. The government didn't want the liability of its upkeep. These gifts to the nation are a two-edged sword, you know. The house, even then, needed millions spending on it and the gardens were completely neglected as no one since Alfred's grandfather had shown any interest in them.'

'What happened to the original paintings?' Cobb asked.

'Ah, well, that's just the thing. No one knows for sure. Of course, the life of an English country squire wasn't what Alfred Latham had in mind for himself at all. He preferred to live on Cap d'Antibes in the south of France, drive a Bugatti, drink champagne for breakfast and spend his evenings in the casino at Monte Carlo. It's always been assumed it was he who commissioned copies and sold the originals to fund his lifestyle.'

'But he had no reason to do that. He owned the paintings — he could do what he liked with them,' Bould said. 'Why would he commission copies and not tell his heir that he had sold the originals?'

'Sergeant, Alfred was a complete eccentric who enjoyed cocking a snook at the world. He probably did it out of devilment.'

'That was an unpleasant thing to do to your own son. He must have been aware of what would happen some day,' Cobb commented. This simply confirmed what he had always suspected about the landed gentry. They were impossible people who seemed to think they could live by their own rules.

William didn't reply. Instead he led the officers round the side of the villa and through a yew arch into the next room. Bounded on all sides by a high hedge with viewing windows cut into it was a long walkway flanked by classical Roman statues in white marble that shimmered in the sun.

'Are these the genuine article?' Cobb asked.

With a shake of his head, William replied, 'Unfortunately not. These are modern replicas we had made. We were lucky enough to have a considerable number of photographs of the garden at the turn of the century, plus the original plans, and there certainly were statues here then. Richard Latham acquired a dozen on his Grand Tour, but they have long since vanished.'

The end of the walkway had been reached

and they passed through another gap in the hedge to find themselves in the Mediterranean garden.

'This is quite amazing,' Bould said. He, at least, was enjoying the gardens — but then he always enjoyed being outdoors. 'And they're a very well-kept secret. I'm surprised you don't publicize them more.'

His words obviously touched a nerve and William bristled. 'I think you'll find we make sure the gardens get all the publicity they can, and don't forget we do a great deal of educational work here. That is one of the main duties the council has, and they discharge it very well, I can assure you.'

'How long have you been employed here?' Cobb asked.

'Just over three years. Ever since we began the restoration work.'

'It must have been very helpful to have a brother who was a councillor.'

If William had been offended by Bould's comments, he was incandescent at Cobb's. Coming to a sharp halt, he wheeled round, churning up a shower of gravel. 'How dare you imply my brother had anything to do with my appointment to this position. I got this job on merit, and merit alone.' Hands clenched at his sides, he was rigid with anger.

Cobb regarded him with interest. 'Calm

down, Mr Boot. I'm sure you did. However, some members of the public might think otherwise.'

'If you mean that little stinker Quentin Makepeace, what's he been saying now? My solicitors have already had to threaten legal action for slander against him, but he never learns.'

Cobb and Bould exchanged glances. 'Who's Quentin Makepeace?' the DI asked.

A short laugh greeted the enquiry. 'Who's Quentin Makepeace?' William echoed, his hands clenching ever tighter. 'He's a trouble-maker, that's who he is. He's always had it in for my brother and me.'

'And why would that be?'

'Jealousy, if you ask me.' Clucking in annoyance, William started to viciously deadhead some Livingstone daisies.

'Jealous of what, exactly?' Bould said.

'Everyone and everything. It's in his nature.' Evasive now, William concentrated on the flowers.

Turning back to their earlier conversation, Cobb said: 'What happened to the son? The one who gave the property away.'

'Do you know, Inspector, I've no idea. He was a doctor in London, that's all I know.'

'One last question: is there any deadly nightshade growing here?'

William's eyes widened. 'Most definitely not! Do you know how toxic that plant is? We have to be most careful over what grows here as these gardens are open to the public.'

They left him in the garden, fussing over the flowers.

'What do we make of him, Sergeant?' Cobb said as soon as they were out of earshot.

'Seemed rather too outraged by suggestions of wrongdoing in his appointment.'

'Didn't he just. Mind you, I think we need to find this Quentin Makepeace and find out just what his gripe is — Now this really is beyond me.'

On William's advice they were taking a circular route back to the car park in order to view all the garden rooms and now they were in a flagged courtyard with an open-sided summer house in the centre and cryptic sculptures dotted around. One was of a tree with human figures blossoming at the tips of the branches. Another was a gigantic egg out of which was hatching a winged horse.

Bould thought they were rather beautiful, but kept his thoughts to himself.

4

In winter the CID room was so cold it was almost unbearable. Now as July wore on it was still unbearable but for completely the opposite reason. All the windows were flung wide open, and the team sat around in open-necked short-sleeved shirts but still baked. Summer had arrived late but with a vengeance.

'Right, gather round, everyone.' Raising his voice as he strode into the room, Cobb commanded immediate attention and everyone swivelled their chairs round to focus on the white board that Bould was busy pinning photographs on.

Taking up a red marker pen, Cobb began scrawling information linking the photographs, speaking as he did. 'Jonathan Boot lived in a very big, expensive house. His wife certainly doesn't buy her clothes at Oxfam, but his company Swallow & Carrick scarcely seems to be raking in the money — so, Ian, your first task is to go through Boot's bank accounts, both personal and professional, with a fine-tooth comb and see what you can find. Rose, I want you to look very closely at

31

William Boot's past. See what qualifications he's got for his current job and what he's done before. He was just a little too indignant about suggestions that his brother might have given him a helping hand. Aaron, see what you can find out about a certain Quentin Makepeace. I want to speak to him as soon as possible.'

'Is he our man?' Aaron asked, drumming the desk with his fingers. A constant fidget, those who were forced to share the CID room with him had at last managed to persuade him to stop jingling the coins in his pocket, but unable to keep still he had now taken to this ceaseless drumming. Sometimes it was possible to recognize a tune in the pattern, but it still drove everybody else to distraction.

'I've no idea,' the DI answered honestly. 'At the moment we have no one in the frame. According to his family, Boot was a man with no enemies other than perhaps Mr Make-peace. It seems that William Boot got his solicitor to come the heavy hand with Makepeace over allegations that the mayor used his influence to get his brother the job at Latham Hall. Now we need to look into this and see if it has any bearing on the case. We'll also interview all his fellow councillors — see what they have to say. Boot may have made some political enemies over the years. Sergeant Bould and I are going to see his solicitor David Bartley — let's see if the will throws up any surprises.'

'Sir,' began DC Rose Cadoxton, 'could it have been accidental? The poisoning, I mean.'

'Not according to Dr Bolton. It can be extracted from deadly nightshade, either by extracting the juice from the berries or by crushing the dried leaves, and it's hard to see why anyone would do that for innocent purposes, and there's no suggestion the mayor committed suicide. Neil and I took a close look at the Boots' garden and there was no deadly nightshade growing there, which again makes accidental ingestion unlikely. Atropine is also used in medicine for certain conditions, none of which applied to Boot, so again accidental overdose can be ruled out. But I'm glad you mentioned it, Rose, because as we don't know in what form the poison was administered we don't know yet what we're looking for. For instance, if we find — and this would be more than our luck's worth — that someone with a known grudge against Boot had deadly nightshade growing in their garden, it wouldn't necessarily give us any evidence that would stand up in court because that's not the only source of atropine and we could be looking for a doctor or nurse with medical supplies.

'Rose, you need to do something else and that's to start to make arrangements for the team to interview all sixty-two councillors — the sooner the better. Aaron, when you're free give Rose a hand. Right, that's it for now.' The team were dismissed with a curt nod and Cobb strode from the room with Bould at his side.

★   ★   ★

David Bartley's office was very different to that of Swallow & Carrick. All gleaming metal and glass, it shouted success and money to all who passed by, let alone ventured inside. He was often described as a smooth operator by those that had come up against him; and he looked exactly that. A sleek shark cruising the rich waters of this particular stretch of Gloucestershire. He was only thirty-three and rumoured to be worth several million. As well as his legal practice he owned many properties in the county, mostly terraced or semidetached houses in towns, all let to students or low-paid workers. Cobb had heard it said that he only just kept on the right side of the licensing laws by making sure the properties came up to the bare legal standards required and nothing more. There were also stories that if tenants fell behind with the rent Bartley had a couple of heavies who saw to it that they paid up pretty quickly or else, but there had never been any formal complaints to the police about this.

They were shown up to the solicitor's office by his PA, who looked as if she had been found on the beach at Marbella. Cobb doubted she'd been hired for her organizational skills.

'Mr Cobb, Mr Bould.' A well-fed, well-dressed man with cold grey eyes and thick black hair, artlessly tousled and gelled into points with the express intention of giving the owner a slightly rebellious look, glanced up from behind a desk the size of a small battleship, but made no effort to stand to greet the officers. 'I understand you wish to speak to me in connection with the late Jonathan Boot. Just how can I help?' He made no offer for them to be seated, so Cobb and Bould pulled up their own chairs to the desk and sat down.

'We're conducting a murder investigation. So let's start with the most obvious of motives. Who gets Mr Boot's money?' Cobb wasn't going to waste words as he had no desire to spend any more time with this man than was absolutely necessary, having taken an instant dislike to him.

'His wife,' Bartley replied immediately. 'They both made wills leaving everything to each other, and then after both their deaths it all goes to their only child, Adam.'

'No other bequests at all?'

'No.' This was emphasized with a firm shake of the head.

'And how much did Mr Boot leave?'

A pause as if the solicitor was considering whether they had overstepped their rights in asking this. 'Roughly two million.'

'That's a lot of money,' Bould said mildly.

'Mr Boot was an astute investor. He had a considerable portfolio of shares and of course his house is worth the best part of a million.'

'Do you also represent Mr William Boot?'

'Yes, as a matter of fact I represent the whole family, but is this relevant? There is the matter of confidentiality to my clients, you know. I hope you're not going to ask me to discuss matters unconnected with my client's death.'

'Have you ever come across a Quentin Makepeace?' Cobb asked, changing the subject abruptly again.

Now the man behind the desk laughed. 'Most people in public office around here have heard of Mr Quentin Makepeace.'

'And why is that?'

'Because he sees the public sector as being

riven with corruption and that his God-given duty is to expose such goings-on. He thinks of himself as the Mary Whitehouse of local democracy.'

'Is it?' Bould glanced up from his notebook. 'Riven with corruption, I mean.'

An expansive gesture was what he received in return. 'Who knows? There are bad apples in every barrel, but I'm not personally aware of anything untoward taking place, and certainly nothing that involves any of my clients,' Bartley ended almost smugly.

'Mr William Boot tells us that he has had to threaten Mr Makepeace with libel action because of allegations his brother got him his job at Latham Hall.'

'I can assure you there is no truth whatsoever in that scurrilous story and I would suggest you do not go around repeating it.'

'You can understand how it might look to an outsider, though,' Cobb responded.

'Mr Boot had no say in his brother's appointment, which was made entirely on his own demonstrable talents.'

'Nevertheless, did Mr Jonathan Boot also feel it necessary to warn Mr Makepeace off?'

'If you mean did I write to him on behalf of both brothers threatening legal action if he did not stop making these allegations, then yes, I did warn Makepeace off.' Bartley glanced down at his watch, a gold Rolex. 'If that's all, gentlemen, I must ask you to excuse me. I have an appointment in Gloucester in forty-five minutes.' He got to his feet and crossed the office.

Cobb remained resolutely glued to his chair, and watched with some amusement as Bartley, realizing he was not being followed, turned back, clearly annoyed to find his word was not being taken as law by The Law. 'If you would just be so good as to give me Mr Makepeace's address,' Cobb said pleasantly, and smiled at Bartley, who stared coldly back.

'I'll get my PA to give you this information, if you don't mind.' The reply was curt, and the door opened in a very pointed manner.

Cobb rose and Bould, taking his cue, did likewise.

Bartley's office led directly into that of his PA's. It was a smaller version of his own, not quite so expensively furnished although it did have fine views over the local park.

'Marilyn, can you find Quentin Make-peace's address for Inspector Cobb? I'm off to Gloucester now and I shan't be back today. If Eric Peasbody rings, tell him the meeting tomorrow is definitely on.' And then he was gone.

Marilyn, who was possibly as old as twenty,

with poker-straight shoulder-length blonde hair, blue eyes and a fake tan which was well shown off in the low-cut short-skirted tight pink dress she was wearing, looked confused, as if she hadn't understood her instructions. As her boss had already disappeared, she turned blankly to Cobb for clarification.

'Mr Quentin Makepeace. I think you'll find his address in Mr Jonathan Boot's file.' Cobb spoke slowly as he thought this was necessary for comprehension.

'Oh, yeah. Right. OK.' She got up and sashayed across the room on six-inch heels. 'Boot, that'll be in the top drawer then,' she said to herself and opened the drawer in question.

The officers watched fascinated as she slowly and laboriously checked through all the files until she came to the right one. Cobb had a feeling that if they could see her face her tongue would be sticking out in concentration.

'Here we are,' she cried in triumph, and waved the file in their faces. Half the contents fell on the floor. 'Whoops, silly me.' One beautifully manicured hand flew to her face and her eyes widened in dismay, but she made no effort to retrieve the papers, preferring to stand there looking helpless.

Cobb guessed she was used to men doing

everything for her as he and his sergeant bent down to gather up the documents. He couldn't believe that such an astute business-man as Bartley would really employ a brainless wonder such as Marilyn. He'd need someone reliable and smart as his secretary. The thought crossed his mind that this girl was a decoy and somewhere else in this building, which was rather on the large side for a single practitioner, the real work was being done by someone quite different. Marilyn was the sort of girl it would be good to parade around the bars and nightclubs, but no one in their right mind would employ her to do any serious work.

'Here we are,' Marilyn crowed and shoved a piece of paper under his nose.

It was a letter from Bartley to Makepeace and Cobb took the opportunity to do more than just take in the address. A quick scan told him the letter was a very threatening one indeed. Bartley didn't pull any punches as he passed on his client's intention to financially ruin the man. He beamed his thanks at the witless secretary as he bid her a heartfelt good day.

5

Rose and Aaron had done their stuff and now the team were busy interviewing all sixty-two Mallerton district councillors, but after a preliminary talk with one in particular, Rose Cadoxton called into the DI's office.

'There's someone I think you should speak to yourself,' she began. 'It's the deputy mayor. There may be nothing in it, but — ' She didn't need to finish.

Cobb trusted her judgement. She was shrewd and he knew she wouldn't be with him for long. Promotion beckoned and then she'd be gone to pastures new. It galled him the way every time he got near enough a perfect team assembled, this happened. It was an impossible situation. He didn't want to hold anyone back, but precisely because they were good they left his team all too quickly and he had to start all over again.

Now he listened as she passed on the details, briefly read her interview notes and then asked her to ring and make arrangements for him and Bould to call.

Later that afternoon the two officers drove out into the Gloucestershire countryside, and headed to Lucknow Farm.

Someone heard the car approach as it bumped its way up what was little more than a rutted track, and the front door of the rambling Victorian farmhouse was thrown open before they came to a halt. An untidy-looking woman, clad entirely in tweeds, came striding down the steps with two Jack Russell terriers fizzing at her heels.

Masie Hintlesham must have been over sixty, but was thin and wiry. She also had a booming voice for such a little person.

'Good to meet you, Inspector, Sergeant. Come in, come in. I've got some tea ready in the drawing room. Trust you'll join me. If not, bad luck, you'll have to watch me eat. Can't miss m'tea. I was born in India — my pa was in the army. Came home after Independence, but always brought up to have afternoon tea. It's a tradition, y'know, and it keeps me going till m'dinner.'

The drawing room was well proportioned and contained a mish-mash of chairs and sofas, sideboards and some other furniture that seemed to have no useful purpose. On a long low table in the middle of the room was arrayed a rather eccentric display of food. Several plates held sandwiches made from bread that had been sawn from the loaf by a profoundly inexpert hand. The slices varied in thickness from at least an inch to nothing at all; where this had happened the fillings could be clearly seen poking through the holes. A lopsided Victoria sponge sat in the centre of the table. Cream and jam were trickling out of the lower side of it.

'Sit yourselves down, no point in being uncomfortable whilst we talk,' Masie said, making it sound more of an order than an invitation. 'And help yourselves to grub. Made it m'self. Bit useless in the kitchen I'm afraid and cooking was never my forte. Always preferred being out with the pigs. Very clean animals, pigs. Not many people know that. Seem to think pigs are dirty — rubbish!'

It wasn't often Cobb was reduced to silence, but he was on this occasion. He was hungry, though, as he was still on the doughnut-free, steamed chicken or fish diet and by now anything was inviting. He decided to risk it.

'These sandwiches are just the job,' the DI said because, to his surprise, they were: thick slices of ham with English mustard and watercress between fresh crusty bread.

Masie flushed with pleasure. 'Cured the ham m'self. You can tell a happy pig from the taste of its meat, y'know. Used to have them dispatched on the farm with their heads in the trough eating away so they never knew what had happened. That's the way to do it. No distress to the animal, y'see. Can't do it now — legislation, y'know. Have to send them to the abattoir instead.' She gave a snort of contempt, making it clear what she thought of the government's view on the way to slaughter pigs.

If it was true that a happy pig made for good-tasting meat, Masie's pigs must have led a life of pure heaven, Cobb decided as he bit into another sandwich.

'Gathered the watercress m'self as well. Grows in the streams all over the estate,' Masie went on, taking a gigantic bite from a real doorstopper.

Having finished his sandwich, which he had enjoyed just a bit too much, the DI eyed the sponge cake. Aware that appearances had already proved deceptive, he decided to try a piece.

'Damn oven,' Masie said viciously, stabbing the cake knife deep into the heart of the sponge. 'Doesn't heat up properly these days. Should get it seen to, I suppose. The door's the problem — it's never shut properly ever since we had the calf in there.'

At this remark, both officers looked startled. Cobb wondered for a moment if she cooked her animals whole.

'No, no,' she said, sensing their misunderstanding as she dished out a slab of broken cake and half-whipped cream onto his plate. Luckily cake forks had been thoughtfully provided. 'Poor thing was rejected by its mother. Been lying out in the rain all night and needed warming up. Didn't want to lose it. It's an old trick. Do it with lambs all the time. Warm them up in a slow oven. Calf's a bit bigger though. Started kicking once it revived. Good sign really — buggered the oven door though.' She looked up and suddenly the façade of an eccentric old woman slipped and Cobb found himself gazing into a pair of shrewd blue eyes the colour of cornflowers. 'But enough of this. You want the dirt on old Jack Boot, don't you?'

'Jack Boot?' said Cobb and waited. He had a feeling that she was going to be a mine of information.

'Jack Boot. Mr Put-the-boot-in. We had plenty of names for the old bugger. None of 'em affectionate.'

'You must have had to work closely with Mr Boot seeing as how you are the deputy mayor this year,' Bould remarked, placing his empty cup and saucer on the table and taking out his notebook now that the pleasantries were over and they were getting down to business.

Masie gave a gruff laugh. 'Not as close as

some, that's for sure.'

'Meaning?' Cobb said quickly, picking up on the implication.

She shot him a no-nonsense look. 'Can't say I ever found Boot attractive but there's no accounting for taste and he'd got the dibs — that's enough for some women — although where from is anyone's guess. It couldn't have been from that clapped-out business of his.'

'Mrs Hintlesham, are you saying Jonathan Boot was having an affair?' It was necessary to be quite clear on this.

'Course he was. You don't think that anaemic wife of his was enough for him? Tried it on with all the women. Even tried it on with me, for God's sake. Didn't try it a second time, I can tell you.'

Privately, Cobb didn't doubt that for a second. Masie Hintlesham was a redoubtable woman. Boot must have been a very brave man. 'Can you supply us with the name of the woman involved?'

'Artemis Dukoy.' Not a moment's hesitation. Masie certainly didn't feel a need to be discreet.

'Isn't she a councillor too?' Bould frowned, trying to place the name.

A snort of derision greeted his question. 'You'd never know it to look at the woman. Thinks she ought to be modelling for *Tatler*, the way she dresses. Like to see her up to her ankles in pig muck.'

'Was this affair common knowledge?' Cobb asked.

Before replying Masie took a large mouthful of cake and they patiently waited for her to eat it. Eventually she said: 'Don't know. It was known to some of our lot, but we never talk to Artemis's lot socially so I've no idea who else knew.'

'When you say our lot and their lot — '

'Artemis's a member of the opposition,' Masie said with great satisfaction, then became severe. 'Don't go in much for cross-party fraternization; don't approve of it, not at all.'

'Did Mrs Boot know about the affair?' said Bould.

'No idea. You'll have to ask her, but I doubt it. Don't they always say the wife's the last to know?'

'Was Mr Boot a racing man?' Cobb said, and noticed that the change of subject didn't faze Masie at all.

'Not to my knowledge. What makes you ask?'

'The name of his house — Foinavon. But perhaps it was the previous occupier's idea.'

'Boot built that house himself. Must have been around 1985 if I remember aright; it was just before he became a councillor, so the name would be his. Bloody apt, I always thought.'

'Why do you say that?'

'Man was a complete chancer. You know the story of how Foinavon won the 1967 Grand National, I take it?' When she saw Bould look doubtful, Masie expounded with relish. Obviously racing was a subject dear to her heart even if the late Jonathan Boot was not. 'Foinavon was a hopeless 'chaser. Not a chance of him winning the National; most thought he wouldn't even finish. His owner didn't even bother turning up to see him run. That's how hopeless the nag was. As it turned out it was because he was so slow he won. Amazing, really, when you think of it.' The thought made her give one of her alarming gruff laughs, more of a 'harrump' really. 'Lots of riderless horses at the front by half-time — always are and they're a complete menace. Anyhow, at the fence after Beechers they decided they'd had enough and stopped. Terrific pile-up followed as the leading riders couldn't avoid crashing into 'em. Those slightly behind the leaders had to slow down to avoid the collision and then hadn't got enough speed to get over the fence. Only horse that managed it was Foinavon — because he was so far behind, his jockey had

48

time to swerve round without losing speed. He jumped the fence from the rails. Went on to win by 200 yards. Never seen anything like it before or since. Odds of 100–1: really annoying thing is the bookies made a killing, because hardly anyone had their money on the horse. The '67 race is known as the Bookies National because of it.'

'Mr Boot must have been well respected as a councillor to be put up as mayor,' Bould said, changing the subject completely.

'Don't be ridiculous! It was simply Buggins' turn,' Masie snorted.

'Buggins' turn? I'd have thought it was an honour to be voted mayor.'

'Don't you believe it! As long as you keep your seat longer than anyone else on the council and behave properly, you get to be mayor. Everyone knows exactly where they are on the list. There's nothing honourable about it. It's my turn next year; that's why I'm deputy now. They're going to break the old girl in gently.'

Cobb decided to return to an earlier remark Masie had made. 'You said no one had an admiring word to say for Mr Boot. Can you explain why that is?'

'He wasn't a gentleman — not pukka at all. He'd got plenty of money, but that didn't make him a gentleman and no one knew where his money came from. His family have lived in Mallerton for yonks and I've known them since the Dark Ages. They're just ordinary folk — his father was the local ironmonger. Boot went away to university in London and returned a rich man. Few years later gets himself elected to the council and before you know it he's running the show. Ruled his party with a rod of iron and was deeply unpleasant to everyone. If Boot could be rude to someone, he would be — apart from the voters, of course. He was no fool and pulled the wool right over their eyes. Public thought he was marvellous, but they didn't know him.'

'So you would say he could have a lot of enemies.'

'Without a doubt.' Then uncertainty seemed to grab her. She ran a hand through already unruly hair. 'Don't think that means anyone disliked him enough to kill him though. Everyone said, 'I could just kill the bastard,' but they don't actually do it.'

'Someone did,' Bould pointed out.

Masie helped herself to another slice of cake and said with gusto: 'It wasn't me and I'll tell you why: I wouldn't have done it at this time of the year. It's downright inconvenient because now I'll have to take over all his duties, and we'll be cutting the rye

50

week after next, all being well. Pity whoever did it couldn't have waited until the autumn when the harvest would be over; wouldn't have minded then.'

'I often find murder is most inconvenient,' said Cobb gravely. Usually such a callous remark would have enraged him, but there was something about Masie Hintlesham that he found quite appealing. He decided it was her down-to-earth honesty and ability to speak her mind regardless of how she came across. For a politician she was amazingly naïve.

6

'We can use this room; I don't want what I have to say to you to be overheard.' Artemis Dukoy wiped her security pass over the lock and led the way into a cupboard of a room furnished only with a round table and two chairs. 'We use this sometimes when constituents come to the council offices to see us.'

Cobb had come alone to see Artemis, as apart from the sheer number of councillors to be interviewed, which meant the rest of his team were being kept busy, he felt she might talk more freely if there was no one else present.

She sauntered across to the table and posed herself very prettily beside one of the chairs, one hand resting lightly on the back, using it as a prop to show herself off and nothing more.

At first sight, Cobb had thought she was in her early thirties and stunningly beautiful, but on closer inspection a better estimate of her age would be nearer fifty. Even he could see that under the thick layer of make-up — skilfully applied, he had to give her that — the smooth skin owed a great deal to the hand of a cosmetic surgeon: the eyes were unnaturally wide and the mouth seemed to be straining at the corners. Nevertheless, she believed in making the most of her assets, which included an amazing dress sense and an hourglass figure. On this occasion she was wearing a pillar-box-red suit tightly cinched in around the waist with a wide green belt. Beneath the above-knee length skirt, long shapely legs were revealed. Cobb had never heard of Jimmy Choo, but he could see her shoes were very expensive all the same. A thick mass of club-cut curly blonde hair ended just below her ears, allowing a pair of long gold drop earrings to catch the afternoon sunlight that poured in through the window behind her.

A greater contrast to Masie Hintlesham would have been hard to find in any council office.

'Do councillors make a habit of eavesdropping on each other?' Cobb enquired.

A silvery laugh greeted his remark. 'My God, yes, they do. I wouldn't trust any of my colleagues as far as I could throw them, and as you see, that wouldn't be very far.'

'And what use do they make of any overheard information?'

'They blog, Inspector, or run to the press, or just put nasty rumours around the town.

53

It's dog eat dog in politics even at this level. The internet is the curse of mankind if you want my opinion.'

'Some people might say keeping the public informed of what their politicians are doing is what democracy is all about.'

'Only those that are gullible or over-idealistic,' she retorted with fire in her voice. Then she composed herself. 'You want to speak to me about Jonathan's death.'

'We're speaking to everyone who had any connection with Mr Boot, and I've been led to understand that you had probably a better connection to him than any of your colleagues on the council.'

She stared at him hard, challenging him, daring him to be more explicit; then she capitulated. 'I could deny it, but there really wouldn't be any point seeing as one of my dear colleagues has obviously already taken great delight in stabbing me in the back from the sound of things. I knew it would happen sooner or later.' She opened her bag and took out a packet of cigarettes before remembering the law. With a sigh of exasperation, the packet was impatiently stuffed back in.

'You weren't that discreet then?'

'Discreet!' Her voice rose an octave. 'This is the council we're talking about. It's an enclosed little world. It's like ancient Rome here with a hundred Caligulas running around, only some of them aren't quite as restrained as the Roman emperor was.'

'Are you married?'

'Yes, actually I am, but my husband and I have what you might call an arrangement.' Distaste at having to discuss her marital situation was evident as she turned away to look out of the window over the roofs of the town.

'This arrangement — can you be more specific?' Cobb felt like being remorseless. Despite the well-used saying that opposites attract, in his experience it was like attracted like. The character of Artemis Dukoy, in turn, was opening a window into the dead man's personality.

She turned back and stared candidly at the DI. 'Look, I'm going to level with you. My husband and I can't stand each other, but both of us would be damaged financially if we divorced, so it suits us very well to stay married and if we console ourselves with other people now and then, there's nothing wrong in it.'

Cobb remained impassive. 'Did it suit Mr Boot very well, or did he take your affair more seriously?'

'Good Lord, no. Jonathan take our affair seriously! You must be joking. It was just a bit of fun for both of us. A dalliance, if you like.'

'Did Mrs Boot know about it?'

The sunshine caught Artemis, bathing her in a golden glow, giving her the look of a celestial being, but her voice was coarse with amusement. 'Do you know, I rather think she did. Sylvia wasn't very interested in that side of things and according to Jonathan she never had been.'

'So he had affairs to compensate but never thought of divorce. Why was that?'

Artemis delved into her bag again and drew out her cigarettes. 'Look, Inspector, if you want to continue this conversation I'm going to have to have a cigarette. Shall we go outside?'

They took a turn around the formal gardens surrounding the council offices. A series of gravel paths meandered round beds edged with low box hedges and filled with a bright display of bedding plants. 'The council are famed for their horticultural displays. The parks department regularly win at Chelsea,' Artemis said, not looking at the beds as she lit up.

'They're very impressive,' Cobb replied. He abhorred smoking and walked slightly upwind of the smoke. 'Now, you were going to tell me about the state of the Boots' marriage.'

Artemis took a long drag on her cigarette, tilting her head back as she filled her lungs before luxuriously exhaling with deep satisfaction. 'Jonathan would never have divorced Sylvia, so it's just as well I didn't want that.'

'Did he ever say why?'

'Not really. He wouldn't talk about it. The only time he came close was once when we'd been at an official function. He'd had quite a lot to drink and afterwards we went on to a private club where he had a lot more. I'd had quite a bit myself and you know how it is. That's the time you start talking much more openly than you would otherwise. Your guard is down. I was bemoaning the fact that Paul — that's my brother — was keen to marry some bimbo he'd picked up in a cheap dive, due entirely to the fact she was half his age and looked good on his arm. I said something about men being very simple really when it came to the women they wanted to marry — all they looked for was a pretty face — and Jonathan sort of smirked and said not him. He had been very, very clever in marrying Sylvia and she was most definitely more than just a pretty face. They were a good team, he said, like Bonnie and Clyde; then he changed the subject and refused ever to discuss it again. I think he regretted ever telling me as much as he did.'

'So you've no idea what he was referring to?'

A shake of the head. 'I've just told you, he wouldn't talk to me about it once he'd sobered up, and it was nothing to do with me so I didn't push it.'

'Thank you, Mrs Dukoy, you've been very helpful,' Cobb said. Although the information was vague it did suggest one thing: the mayor wasn't quite the fine upstanding pillar of society he had liked to portray himself as being.

★ ★ ★

Later that day, the DI called the team together in the CID room for a brainstorming session.

On entering the room, the air hit him like a blast furnace.

'Can't we run to some fans?' he grumbled, removing his jacket and tie and loosening his collar.

'We've asked, but there's no money in the budget,' Rose said.

'What do they cost — thirty pounds?' Cobb dug his hand in his pocket. 'I'll pay for the bloody thing myself. Go out and get one as soon as I've finished here.' He handed some notes to Rose. 'Don't think I've gone soft on you, but it isn't going to help my investigations if you're falling asleep whilst I'm talking. Now tell me what you've found out.'

The reports brought back from the interviews made for depressing hearing.

'Right: all we seem to have found out is that Boot was universally disliked by his colleagues but everyone's sticking to the story that it was just because he had an unpleasant personality. God help us if this ever becomes a motive for murder. Half the population would be dead.

'However, I have come across a piece of information that may, or may not, be of relevance. Councillor Artemis Dukoy was having an affair with Boot and when he was bottled one night he let the following slip.' Cobb proceeded to tell his team what he had learnt in the council offices gardens. 'The reference to Bonnie and Clyde suggests some sort of criminal activity, I think you'll agree. Now, we can ask Mrs Boot directly about it but she's hardly likely to admit to whatever it is, so we'll start going through Boot's affairs with a fine-tooth comb.

'My gut instinct tells me money is going to play a big part in this investigation. There's some reason why he called his house Foinavon — a horse who came in at 100–1 when he won the National. Now Boot went to London an impecunious student and came back a rich man. We need to know how this happened.'

'Perhaps he just got lucky on the horses,' Aaron said.

Cobb scratched his nose. 'It's possible, but even at odds of 100–1 you'd need to stake a hell of a lot of money to make enough to buy land and build a big detached house, even in those days, and as Boot was only nineteen when Foinavon won the National, where would he have got his stake money from?'

'He could have been a professional gambler who started small and built up his winnings over the years. Say Foinavon was his first bet; because of the odds even a small wager would have produced large winnings. He could have gone on from there,' Bould suggested.

'Perhaps, but if he found he could make easy money from gambling why give it up to become a surveyor? Once a gambler, always a gambler. They get an adrenalin rush from betting; I can't see anyone getting that from doing a house survey. No, from what I've heard about the man, I think the name was his way of making a sly joke, of sticking two fingers up at the rest of the world. Councillor Hintlesham called Boot a chancer, and I want to know why.

'Ian, get the company books from Swallow & Carrick — let's see just how well that firm is doing. I think Boot and his partner were at loggerheads over something and I want to know what that was. Neil, come with me. We're going to talk to this Quentin Makepeace — let's see what he's got to say for himself.'

★ ★ ★

The letterbox rattled as the mail dropped through. Halfway down the stairs, Sylvia froze. Her nerves were in shreds. Every day brought a new threat. Adam was beginning to question why she never went out any more — for the moment she could plead grief but this couldn't go on. As long as he was around she felt safe but she couldn't keep him by her side forever. Luckily he worked for himself and so could stay here as long as she needed him — but that might be for the rest of her life and sooner or later he would go back to London. Thank God for computers and email. Modern technology meant he could work anywhere, which made it harder for him to leave. So far, every time he mentioned returning to the capital she managed to talk him out of it, but for how much longer? And when he went, then what was she going to do? What could she do? It was the helplessness of her situation that traumatized her so much.

There on the carpet, a cream deckle envelope taunted her. It was just a piece of paper but to her it was as if a primed grenade had been lobbed through the letterbox. Her fingers tightened around the banister rail. She felt dizzy with fear. The thought crossed her mind that she should go to the police, but that thought was instantly dismissed. How could they do anything to help when she didn't know who the sender was — or why they wanted her dead?

7

48 Poppyfield Cresent was a neat 1930s semi in a row of neat 1930s semis. There was nothing to distinguish it from three dozen others in the quiet leafy sweep of road.

A tall, rangy man was pushing a lawn-mower over the grass at the front of his house. His lined and leathery face suggested a lifetime spent outdoors and although he looked in his sixties, he boasted a full head of brown hair making him look more vital than his stooped posture suggested.

'Quentin Makepeace?'

The man looked up as DI Cobb hailed him. 'Yes, I am Mr Makepeace. And you are?'

Cobb introduced himself and Bould, noticing that Makepeace seemed more annoyed than concerned.

'Look, if that Bartley fellow has been complaining about me to the police I won't stand for it. I've had more than enough of him.'

'Mr Bartley hasn't asked us to contact you, but we do want to talk to you about Jonathan Boot — ' Cobb didn't get any further. He'd lit a firework and could only watch in fascination as Makepeace began to fizz and spark all over the lawn.

'That man will be the death of me,' Makepeace spluttered.

'Really? That's interesting considering it's his death we want to discuss.'

'I meant Bartley. Boot was a nasty piece of work, but his solicitor is nothing but a Shylock. He's determined to have his pound of flesh from me, but it will be comprised of my beating heart.'

'Yes, we understand you had accused Mr Boot of some impropriety and he was threatening to sue you for defamation.'

'That's putting it mildly. Boot and his solicitor were out to ruin me. That's what people like them do. That's how they put a stop to effective scrutiny of their actions. They go all out to destroy you.'

'Then you should take heart in the knowledge that a dead person can't be libelled, so any action Mr Bartley intended on behalf of his client will now end.'

Makepeace eyed Cobb incredulously. 'And that's supposed to make me happy? Boot's got away with it but now he's dead there's an end to everything — I don't think so. There's still his brother William who is every bit as vindictive as the late lamented Jonathan.'

'I'm curious to know why there is such bad

blood between you and the Boots. Can you tell me what this is all about?'

Makepeace kicked the mower as if he blamed it for all his troubles. 'Come inside. The neighbours will be enjoying this if no one else is.' He slouched moodily towards the front door, which was ajar to allow the electric cable for the mower through.

Cobb and Bould exchanged looks and followed, hopping over a small border fringing the lawn containing a lot of poor soil and several stunted rose bushes, interspersed with a few straggly marigolds.

Inside the house was cool and dark after the blistering heat of the day, and the change in temperature seemed to have a beneficial effect on Makepeace's temper.

'Shall we go into the front room? We might as well make ourselves comfortable if you really want to hear this sorry tale,' Makepeace said over his shoulder as he took them into a room both austere and nondescript, lacking any sign of a female touch. One glance told the officers there was no Mrs Makepeace in residence. They sat in old but solid battered brown leather chairs.

Bould took out his notebook and waited.

A silence grew as Makepeace seemed to be having second thoughts about giving them an explanation of his actions towards the Boots, and in the end Cobb had to prompt him to begin.

'Can you please tell us why the Boot brothers were threatening to sue you for defamation?'

Makepeace rubbed his temple, and then seemed to have decided upon a particular role to play. 'I'm just a concerned member of the public doing my duty, which is to make sure our elected guardians of democracy don't abuse their position and squander taxpayers' money.'

'Very commendable, sir,' said Cobb, still keeping an impassive face.

'Thank you. That's how I see it. Anyway, I have my concerns about Mr Boot. You will be aware, no doubt, that his brother has been appointed to a very lucrative post at Latham Hall. It is my contention that he has no qualifications or experience that make him suitable for the post and therefore the only conclusion one can draw is that he got the job through his brother's intervention.'

'Have you any proof of this?'

'No, sadly. The mayor and his brother are two of a kind. They are both devious and far too astute to get caught out.'

'Then don't you think it is rather rash of you to go around making the type of allegations you have been making? A law suit is inevitable.'

'Oh, I'm not so sure Councillor Boot would have been that keen to pursue legal action against me. You see, there are one or two other things in his past.' Makepeace threw back his head and stared at the DI, but his look was enigmatic and his words cryptic.

'Such as?'

'There was a very big retail park built a few years ago just outside the town. The land was sold to the developers for something around four million pounds. It was green belt land and a very large opposition was mounted against this pristine farmland being built on, and although the council's own officers recommended refusing, it went before the planning committee and lo and behold, permission was granted.'

'What's that got to do with Councillor Boot?' Bould asked, looking up.

There was a certain grim satisfaction on Makepeace's face as he explained. 'Councillor Boot was the chairman of the planning committee at the time.'

'Are you suggesting some impropriety there?' Cobb said.

'There were a lot of occasions when Councillor Boot called in building applications — that means the planning committee make the final decision and can override their paid officers' opinions, even though one might question whether trained and experienced planners know more than councillors on such matters. In many cases where the officers recommended refusal the committee voted in favour of development.'

'But if the committee voted in favour then it wasn't just down to Mr Boot's decision.'

Makepeace smiled at the DI as if he thought him naïve. 'No, but he had stuffed the committee with his men who would vote as directed by him. Either that or backhanders were involved,' he explained patiently, as if to an idiot.

Cobb decided enough was enough. 'Mr Makepeace, whilst I have no doubt you honestly believe what you are saying, unless you can actually back your words up with facts I strongly advise you to desist from expressing your opinions in public. Do you have any proof of any of this?'

Still unshakeable, Makepeace replied, 'I've already told you, neither of the Boot brothers are fools. They're far too clever to get caught out. But I would suggest that you take a very close look at the late mayor's finances and ask yourself where his money comes from and how he can afford to live the lifestyle he does.'

'We have every intention of doing just that.' Cobb rose to his feet. He disliked being told how to do his job, particularly by a man who seemed high on obsession but low on facts. 'We'd just like a look round your garden before we go. I take it you have no objections?'

'No, of course not.' If he was surprised by the request, he didn't show it.

'Good. Perhaps you'll lead the way.'

They went through the house, into a narrow kitchen and out of the back door and into blinding sunlight.

After the cool dark interior, it took a moment for the officers' eyes to adjust. There wasn't much to see, just another rectangle of badly kept lawn surrounded by narrow borders of poor soil with a few perennials and shrubs listlessly fighting to survive, and a small shed at the far end.

'As you can see, I'm not much of a gardener,' Makepeace said apologetically.

A quick glance was enough to show there was no deadly nightshade growing in the small garden. 'I take it you're retired?' Cobb asked as he and Bould made their way out through the little ornamental gate closing off the narrow passage between the house and the wall of the next-door property.

'Yes, I finished work about two years ago.'

It was strange what hobbies people took up when they retired. Whatever else he did, when the time came, Cobb had no intention of becoming the caped crusader of local democracy. Still, it took all sorts.

'What was your occupation?' Bould asked.

'I was a missionary.'

It wasn't often people's occupations surprised the DI, but this was one of those times. Whether it was just because the term sounded so old-fashioned or whether it was due to his atheist beliefs, he was surprised to hear such an occupation still existed. 'Were you abroad for many years?'

'Yes, all my adult life, but I wanted to come back to die in Gloucestershire. It's a strange thing how the call of one's place of birth gets louder the older one gets. There's no one left here now that I remember, or who would remember me, but I feel comfortable here. I belong.'

'What on earth do we make of him?' Bould said as they crossed the narrow street to where their car was parked.

'The fact he's a God botherer explains everything,' Cobb replied morosely as he climbed into the passenger seat. 'Probably thinks he's got the Almighty's blessing to annoy the councillors. You can never reason with that sort.' He checked his watch. It was nearly six. 'Let's get back to the station double quick. I'm going to have to get away early tonight.'

'Doing something special, sir?' Bould put the car into gear and pulled out from the kerb into the deserted road.

'Sarah and I are going to a concert at Chawlton Hall.'

'Ah.' Bould didn't need to say anything more. He knew the love of classical music was exclusively on the distaff side of the marriage.

'You may well say 'ah', Sergeant, but as it happens I am quite looking forward to this. It's outdoors, by the lake: Mozart and Chopin — now I can cope with them because they're tuneful. It's the modern stuff I can't stand.'

'And it's a fine night. Are you taking a picnic hamper?'

The mention of food sunk Cobb into an immediate gloom. 'Apparently, but I've no say in what's in it.'

'Cholesterol still not normal, sir?'

'So I'm told.' The annoying thing was he felt as fit as he had when he was a young man.

'I'm sure whatever Mrs Cobb has packed will be delicious.'

The DI shifted in his seat and eyed his sergeant suspiciously, but as Bould kept a straight face he was forced to take the remark at face value. 'Hmm. It may well be delicious to some but not necessarily to me. Time was,

71

and not that long ago, when all good coppers survived on nothing but a diet of beer, fags and pies and chips. Now look at us. It's the nanny state saying it knows what's best for us, but I think I know what's best for me.'

'You'll live longer this way.'

'But do I want to? Ever heard the old joke about the man who goes to his doctor and asks how to live to be a hundred?' When he received a shake of the head in reply, Cobb continued. 'The doctor says, 'Give up cigarettes, alcohol and women.' The man says, 'And I'll live to be a hundred?' and the doctor replies, 'No, but it'll feel like it'.'

The punchline was delivered with such gloom that it was clear Bould was not meant to laugh, or indicate in any way that he found this funny, and so the rest of the drive back to the station was conducted in silence.

8

'There you are.' Adam Boot came running lightly down the broad, shallow steps leading from the little patio area in front of the French windows and onto the lawn.

His mother looked up at him with difficulty. She was kneeling on the grass, vigorously weeding a circular rose bed, a trowel in one hand and an old battered straw hat with a wide brim shading her eyes and nearly touching her nose.

'I've got to go into Gloucester. My laptop's playing up and I need to get it fixed immediately.'

'Must you?' It was impossible for Sylvia to keep her dismay to herself.

'I shan't be long, Mother — no more than a couple of hours, and you're occupied here. That's good. I'm glad you're taking an interest in the garden again. You always did have green fingers. Why don't you bring some of those roses into the house? You could do an arrangement for the hall. It'd make the place seem a bit more cheerful — more like a home should be.'

Sylvia pushed her hat out of her eyes with

the back of her hand so she could give her son a long hard look. 'I don't know why you should care what this place looks like. You hardly ever come down here any more, so don't try to pretend Foinavon means anything to you. If your father hadn't died you wouldn't be here now.'

It took an effort for Adam to swallow back the sigh that rose within him. 'Please don't start this again, Mother. It's not that I don't want to visit, it's finding the time. Like most people, I have to work for a living. Tell you what, why don't we go out to dinner tonight? My treat. Book somewhere really nice.' He bent down and kissed her cheek. 'Bye!' And he was gone before she could protest further.

There had been another letter that morning, and she wasn't taking any chances. Left alone out here with no neighbours for half a mile, she felt like a sitting duck. Suppose the writer of those hateful letters came to the house — she'd be at their mercy with no chance of calling for help.

Steady on, girl. Pull yourself together. She couldn't go on like this for the rest of her life. Perhaps she would go to the police; after all, she'd got nothing to hide. She'd done nothing wrong. Well, not for a very long time, she mentally corrected herself, and it was only the one bad thing. There were lots of people who spent their entire lives doing bad things, so she was better than them. It was so long ago she never gave it much thought these days, and besides, there couldn't be anyone left alive who knew, so even if she went to the police they could never find out what she'd done.

Perhaps she'd go now, whilst Adam was out. She'd die if he ever found out what she'd done, so this was a good time. Quickly gathering up her trowel and weeding bucket, she got to her feet and made for the compost heap at the bottom of the garden, screened from the house by a tall yew hedge.

'Oh!' She pulled up sharp. Her heart began to pound wildly as she rounded the hedge and saw someone standing, waiting. 'What are you doing here? What do you want?' Turning in blind panic to flee, calling in vain for her son, she got no further than a yard before she was cut down.

★   ★   ★

'Who found her?' Cobb asked, taking in the fallen figure.

The new pathologist, Dr Bolton, looked up from his examination of the body. 'Her son. He's in the house now in a state of shock.'

Sylvia Boot was lying on her back across

75

the compost heap. Her face was livid, and suffused with blood. A ligature had all but disappeared into the folds of her neck.

'She was strangled — well, garrotted if you want to be precise,' Bolton informed him in an ill-tempered way which, Cobb was beginning to realize with a sinking heart, was his usual disposition. He was a middle-aged man whose lachrymose face bore the expression of one who was dissatisfied with the cards life had dealt him. Bolton's reputation had preceded him and it appeared he made a habit of falling out with everyone he worked with. Now he pulled back the rolls of flesh so that the officers could see the thick band of green string that had ended Sylvia's life. 'It looks like garden twine to me.'

'Any idea yet on time of death?'

'The son went off to Gloucester at ten past one. He returned at 3.40 and found her like this. So there's your time limits.'

'Providing the son's telling us the truth,' Cobb said. 'I'd like a totally accurate time in order to rule him out, provided he can prove he was in Gloucester when he says he was.'

The pathologist looked even more displeased than he had previously, and spoke grudgingly. 'I could get the eyeball potassium level test done, if you really want me to. It's very expensive and we've been told to keep expense to the minimum.'

The last thing Cobb wanted was a lecture in good housekeeping from the pathologist. Didn't he get one every day from the chief superintendent? Every police officer in the country knew the budget constraints were being tightened mercilessly. The pathologist was not in charge of this investigation; he was. 'Yes, I do want it done. Is the son fit to be interviewed?' He turned away from the body, taking no pleasure in looking at the lifeless husk of a once-living being. Not for the first time, the DI wondered how it was that any normal person could want to make a career out of cutting up corpses.

'You can try, but I doubt you'll get a lot of sense out of him. As I said, he seems very shocked.'

'Right then — we'll go and try. Come along, Sergeant.'

They went into the house by the French windows and found Adam Boot pouring himself a very large gin and tonic. His hand was shaking so much the bottle clinked heavily against the cut-glass tumbler and he eyed the officers wildly. When he spoke it was in a voice thick with emotion. 'You'll have to excuse me. I've never seen a dead body before, and it was my mother's.'

'We're very sorry about what has happened

here, and I know this is a far from good time, but it's important for us to ask you a few questions if you feel up to it,' Cobb said gently.

'Of course.' Adam set his drink down untouched.

'You found your mother, we understand.'

'Yes.' The memory caused him to shut his eyes and a shudder passed through his body. 'I'd gone in to Gloucester. My laptop was playing up and I needed to get it fixed. When I left she was fine. She was weeding the rose bed. I said I wouldn't be long and that was the last time I saw her.' A sob rose in his throat and was choked back.

'What time did you leave the house?'

There was a long pause whilst Adam struggled for self-control. 'It was just after lunch. About five, ten past one. I can't be more certain than that.'

'And she was alone at the time?'

'Yes.' Now the drink was taken up and knocked back in one, but did nothing to restore the colour to his skin.

Cobb considered how to ask the next question without alarming the young man. 'Mr Boot, someone has killed both your parents within the last week. Can you think of anyone with a grudge against them who would wish to do this?' What was worrying the DI was the possibility that the killer intended wiping out the whole family, one by one. He hoped that possibility hadn't occurred to Adam.

'No, no, I can't.' The denial was vigorous; the voice rising. 'But I think my mother was frightened of someone.'

Cobb felt that familiar quickening of his pulse. 'Why do you say that?'

As if aware that he needed to keep his wits about him, Adam took a deep breath, ran his fingers through his hair, and became visibly calmer. 'She was very keen for me to stay with her at all times, and she didn't want to go out of the house, and she had received some letters. She didn't realize I saw her face when the postman delivered them. Then I found their burnt remains in the grate. They had frightened her, but I don't know what they said.'

'Did you ask her about these letters?'

'Yes, but she denied receiving anything untoward. She said that after what had happened to Father it was hardly surprising she felt nervous. She insisted it was some sort of maniac who had killed him.'

'Really? Now that's a very interesting conclusion to come to,' Cobb said. 'A maniac. I wonder why she thought that.'

'I'd have thought it obvious. Why would

any sane person want to kill my father?'

'Ah, Mr Boot. That's just what we intend finding out. To your knowledge, has anything been taken from the house?'

In response he got a doubtful shake of the head. 'I don't think so, but I haven't really had a look.'

'I take that to mean there's been no obvious sign of a disturbance. We'll take a look round before we go. I'd particularly like to see your parents' bedroom and I assume you have no objections?'

'No, course not — you've got your job to do.'

They left him in the lounge, measuring out another large gin.

'Nice house,' Cobb observed, gazing around him as they passed through the hallway.

'Impersonal, though. It wouldn't be my choice. It's like something out of *Ideal Homes*,' Bould replied.

'I rather think that's the idea. It's somewhere to impress your enemies and friends alike,' Cobb said as they climbed the staircase to a half landing. From here a huge window gave views over the garden to the fields beyond. In the distance the hazy outline of the Cotswold hills beckoned.

The stairs turned back on themselves for

the final flight to the first floor and off a long, wide landing several doors opened. The first one they tried led into what appeared to be a dressing room, and the second into a double room that contained only masculine items and therefore, they reasoned, was Adam's room.

Further along, they found an en-suite room of vast proportions. A silk floral dressing gown hung from a hook on the back of the door, and the dressing table was littered with perfume bottles and make-up.

Cobb went straight over to the dressing table and started opening drawers, whilst Bould checked out the chest of drawers. After that they moved methodically and carefully through the room, checking everything, looking under the bed, pulling out furniture, lifting bed linen.

They found nothing during their search, but Bould did notice something was missing.

'Look at this, sir,' he said, pointing to the sea-green bedroom wall. Sunlight fell across it in great flat slabs and the change of colour, although slight, was easily seen.

Turning away from his search of the wardrobe, the DI walked over to stand beside his sergeant. 'Yes. There's been a picture hanging here — you can see the outline where the sun's faded the paint around, and there are the two holes where a picture hook would have been. The question is when and why was it removed.'

'Do you think that's what the killer was after?' Bould's eye travelled down the wall and came to a halt on something bright and shiny half hidden in the carpet pile. He stooped to retrieve it, holding it out for his boss to see.

Cobb took the pin and inserted it in one of the holes. It fitted perfectly. 'Someone removed whatever hung here in a hurry. So it might well have been. Let's go and talk to the son again. See if he can shed any light on this.'

He was where they'd left him, still at the little drinks table with a glass of gin in his hands, although they couldn't tell if it was the one he had been holding when they left or another one.

Cobb hoped he wasn't too far gone to be of assistance to them. 'Mr Boot, there appears to be a picture missing from your parents' bedroom wall. We need to know what has happened to it.'

'Hmm?' Lost in thought, Adam only just seemed aware of the officers' presence. He took another gulp of his drink. 'No idea. I haven't been in my parents' bedroom often since I was a child. They were quite strict about that sort of thing. I had a lot of talk about 'boundaries' and not crossing them when I was growing up.'

'Well, can you tell us anything about the picture? Do you remember it hanging there when you were a child?'

Frowning in concentration, Adam took his time to consider this. 'I do remember there used to be a painting there of Tewkesbury Abbey — some sort of sentimental Victorian thing if I recollect, but that doesn't mean it was there yesterday. My parents liked to have paintings around the house — as you can see.' He gestured at the paintings festooning the walls. 'Not that they were really interested in art for art's sake. Pictures were used by my mother as fashion accessories to go with the rest of the room's furnishings. Consequently, they never paid a lot for what they bought. Junk shops, second-hand shops, little auction houses was where they would go to pick up something that would go with that year's look. Then, when the interior design gurus said a particular look was passé and something else was in, my mother would redecorate and chuck out all the accessories, including the furniture and paintings. If she'd paid more than a hundred pounds for a particular piece she might put it back to auction, but otherwise they went to charity shops. Very hot on charity was my mother, as long as it didn't start at home.' A dark smile accompanied the last words. The drink seemed to be making Adam dwell on personal grievances.

Cobb made a mental note to explore the Boots' home life further, but for the moment he kept himself focused on the painting. 'So, that painting could have been removed at any time in the past what, ten, fifteen years?' Only it couldn't have been that long because if Mrs Boot redecorated as often as her son implied, the darker rectangle of wall would have been painted over long ago and the pin hoovered up. The fact that the pin was still on the carpet suggested to him that the painting must have been removed very recently.

'Correct.'

Cobb pushed the point. 'And to your knowledge it was a view of Tewkesbury Abbey.'

'Yes, but as I said that was then, and it might not have been there now.'

'But wouldn't your parents have replaced it with another?' Bould asked. 'From what you've said I would have assumed that would be the case.'

Adam shrugged his shoulders. 'Possibly.' His attitude made it clear he could see no connection between the painting and his parents' death.

'Do you have a key to the house?'

The change of direction in Cobb's questionings surprised the young man. 'Of course I do. This is my family home, after all.'

'And did you have to use it to get back in on your return this afternoon?'

Enlightenment swept across Adam's face. 'Yes, because I came in through the front door, which was locked, but the French windows were open — although that's no more than I expected as Mother was in the garden.'

'So whoever killed your mother could have gained easy access to the house?' This confirmed Cobb's theory that the killer could have taken the painting.

'Yes — yes, you're right. Anyone could have done that. But I don't know who would want to.' He spread his hands in a helpless gesture. 'I don't know why anyone would want to kill my parents.'

Seeing Adam was beginning to fall apart, Cobb moved briskly to the business side of things: 'We're treating the house as a crime scene. You'll need to find somewhere else to stay for the night, Mr Boot. I'll get an officer to drive you to wherever you need to go. Sergeant, get the SOCO boys in here and tell them to concentrate on the bedroom. It's hoping for too much, but there's always the chance the killer took the painting and left a fingerprint.'

* * *

'Right, let's consider what we've got. Anyone want to start the ball rolling?' Cobb was addressing his team in front of the white board on which photographs of the victims and what scant information they had come by were displayed.

His team variously stood or sat around in a horseshoe, frowning in concentration.

'There seems to be some sort of garden connection,' Rose began tentatively. 'I know it sounds crazy but Mr Boot was poisoned with atropine which comes from deadly night-shade and his wife was strangled with garden twine and Mr Boot's brother works at Latham Hall . . . ' She trailed off in uncertainty.

'We've not going to rule anything out at this stage, however crazy it sounds,' Cobb replied, encouraging her.

Bould took up the theme and carried it further. 'Latham Hall might come into it. They received a Lottery grant of ten million pounds; that's a lot of money by anyone's standards and Quentin Makepeace was vehement in his belief that Councillor Boot was corrupt. Could this be about money — some sort of financial swindle?'

'That's definitely a line of enquiry we need to pursue. Aaron, see what qualifications William Boot has for his job at Latham Hall and find out what he did before. Makepeace believes he couldn't have got the job fairly, which in itself is interesting. We might ask ourselves how Makepeace could know this? He says William had no suitable qualifications but I'd like to know how a member of the public could find that out. Job applications are confidential, so unless there is a mole in the council's personnel department, he couldn't be privy to such information.

'Now today there's a little matter of a painting that might, or might not, be missing.' He quickly sketched out for the team the findings earlier in the day. 'SOCO are still going through the house, but there were no fingerprints in the bedroom other than Mr and Mrs Boot, and those belonging to a Mrs Eddie Darley, who cleaned for them and who has confirmed there was a painting of a 'big church' on the wall. The son doesn't think the picture had any value and we don't know exactly when it was removed as Eddie only comes once a week, so it may have absolutely nothing to do with his parents' murders but we need to keep its disappearance in mind.

'We also need to concentrate on where the atropine came from and how Boot managed to digest it. If it was slipped into his food or drink, which at the moment is the supposition, then that has to mean someone close to him. The toxicology report is back and confirms the presence of a large quantity of atropine in Boot's body. Dr Bolton tells me that it would have been administered about three hours before Boot died.'

'Three hours? That's a long time for poison to take effect, isn't it?' asked Rose.

'Apparently atropine is absorbed through the gut and not the stomach, hence the delay. This means we can say with some certainty that Boot must have ingested the poison at around midday.'

'I've been thinking about why the killer chose this particular poison,' Bould began and everyone turned to look at him in expectation. 'Atropine is named after Atropos, one of the three Fates who chose how and when a person would die. I wondered if there was any significance in it.'

'So are we looking for an Oxford university professor?' DC Aaron Walker enquired with a certain amount of sarcasm.

'No piece of information is wasted, even if we don't know what to do with it at the time,' his boss reminded him. 'Although I don't like killers who are that clever; they're the ones who want to play games with us and give us the runaround. Bearing in mind we've now had two murders in just over a week, that's not a prospect I relish.'

'It's too early in the year for deadly nightshade to have produced any berries, isn't it?' Rose said.

'The juice could have come from last year's berries,' Ian Constable suggested.

'But that would suggest the killer has bided his time for nearly a year, and I don't know why anyone would do that. If that was the case, it would suggest a restraining factor about which we know nothing.' Cobb preferred not to go down that road — it was too speculative and they had little enough in the way of solid facts as it was. 'Alternatively, as I've already said, atropine is used in medicine and most doctors would have access to a medically prepared solution.

'At the moment, I'd rather concentrate on how the poison got into Boot's system. The fact that he went about his usual business right up until the time he died means he had no reason to suspect anyone had tampered with his food. I come back to my earlier point: that means it is most likely someone he knew. It was certainly someone who had access to him and so Rose, Aaron, your next task is to check back on where, when and what he ate or drank around midday on the day he died. Find out who was around at the time that might have had the opportunity. Bould and I will concentrate on motive.

'Ian, have you had any joy with Boot's finances?'

'I've had a preliminary look at his bank accounts, but there's been no unusual or irregular transactions — just his councillor allowances every month, plus income from savings accounts.'

There was something about the way he said the last five words that caught everyone's attention. He left a theatrical pause before continuing. 'Every month two thousand pounds went in from various deposit accounts. That's twenty-four thou a year and bearing in mind the low rate of interest at the moment, plus the tax he'd have to pay on it, I reckon he's got to have getting on for a million in deposit accounts alone.'

'Has he, by God!' exclaimed the DI. 'And somehow I don't think it's come from Swallow & Carrick. I know his solicitor said he'd got investments of around a million but I took that to mean stocks and shares — that's what investments usually means, not money in deposit accounts. So is this another source of income that even Bartley didn't know anything about?'

'Could Swallow & Carrick be a front?' Bould said. 'Peter Smith seemed genuine, but he could be the fall guy.'

'Anything's possible. Ian, start going through the deposit accounts and see what you can find. Boot didn't come from a wealthy family — his dad was the local ironmonger — so where did he get his money from? Boot went off to London in the late seventies and came back to Mallerton a rich man, which means he made it *before* he joined Swallow & Carrick, so no, he didn't get rich from the day job.'

9

The letter made no sense whatsoever. Adam stared at it, turned it over in his hands to see if there was a clue on the back. Nothing. He picked up the cream deckle envelope and doubled checked to make sure it was addressed to him. It was. His name and address in neat black capitals formed a block in the middle of the envelope. He looked again at the single piece of paper he had taken out. It had been folded twice to fit the envelope. It was the sort of white A4 paper that could be bought in any stationers that sold paper for computer printers. There was no writing on it but glued onto the sheet were two words.

Your next.

Because the spelling of 'you're' was wrong he hadn't understood it at first. Then realization hit him and filled him with fury and fear in equal measure. He crumpled up the page, his lips set in a tight thin line. He knew exactly what he was going to do.

★ ★ ★

There were three men in the DI's office, Cobb, Bould and Adam Boot, and all their attention was focused on the paper lying on his desk.

Pointing a finger at the sheet, but careful not to touch it, Cobb said: 'When did this arrive, Mr Boot?'

'In the post this morning. It came in this.' Adam handed over the envelope.

'We'll need to keep both of them for now.' The envelope was carefully picked up by a corner and deftly inserted into the clear plastic bag Bould was holding open. 'And we'll need to take your fingerprints for elimination purposes.' The chances of any prints being found on either pieces of paper were unlikely but it had to be done. The words had been cut out of a newspaper and crudely stuck in the middle of the sheet. 'This sounds like an explicit threat from our killer, and we'll offer you police protection, of course. Do you have any idea why someone would want to kill you?'

Adam shook his head. 'You asked me yesterday if I knew of any reason why anyone would want to kill my parents, and I said no. Threatening me makes even less sense. I've lived in London for the past ten years. I'm a website designer; I don't move in the same circles as my parents. I can't think of anyone I know who would know them.' He was both worried and perplexed. Edginess made it difficult for him to keep still and he moved around the room as he talked. 'I think I'll go back to London if it's all the same to you. I'd feel safer there. I'd rather not have some plod — sorry, no offence — following me around all the time, so I'll decline your protection offer for the time being.'

Cobb wasn't happy with this but he couldn't force Adam to take his advice. 'Very well, if that's what you are sure you want but if you change your mind at any time just let us know. We'll need your contact details in London, and my sergeant here will take a statement from you regarding this letter and take your prints at the same time.' If he wasn't going to have any protection it was best the young man didn't stay in Mallerton, and it was possible that the letter had been sent with the sole intention of scaring him away. 'One thing occurs to me. You said your mother received letters that upset her. I don't suppose you are able to say if they were the same as this one?'

'I'm sorry, I can't tell. I only saw her read them at a distance.' Adam took a step closer and gazed at Cobb with candour. 'I thought I knew my parents but there's something in their lives that I realize now I wasn't party to.

I want to know what it is. I want to know why they were killed.'

'So do we, Mr Boot. So do we. Now if you'd be so kind as to follow Sergeant Bould, he'll take you down to an interview room for the formalities.'

★   ★   ★

When Bould had finished with Adam, he returned to his boss's office via the canteen. He had a feeling Cobb would appreciate his actions.

He was right.

'Good man. Grab yourself a coffee and park yourself down.' Cobb was poring over a photocopy of the letter and envelope, the originals now on their way to Forensics — and a mug of coffee steamed gently beside them.

Putting the plate of doughnuts in the centre of the desk, Bould pulled up a chair.

'See, what we need to work out is this: does the use of the word 'your' instead of 'you're' mean the killer isn't very literate, or is it a deliberate attempt to mislead us?' Cobb stabbed at the word with one hand, as he picked up a doughnut with the other.

His sergeant picked up the copy of the envelope and looked at the neatly written address. 'This has been written with a fountain pen. There's not many people use them these days.'

'Quite. That suggests someone literate and educated.'

'Or snobbish?' Bould made it a question. 'You know, someone keen on etiquette.'

'You mean a member of the landed gentry.' The DI's tone conveyed his feelings on them very clearly.

'Not necessarily. What about an older person? When did they stop using fountain pens in school? I remember my father having something to say when he discovered me doing my homework in biro. I had something of a lecture on the subject.'

'An older person.' The first doughnut was finished. To hell with his cholesterol; there were far more dangerous things a policeman faced in the course of his duty. He picked a second one, this time the one with chocolate icing. Sarah would never know. It was probably steamed fish for dinner tonight. He almost groaned out loud. After chewing for several seconds, Cobb said, 'Boot was sixty-one and his missus fifty-eight, so this could be a contemporary of theirs.'

'The handwriting is very neat and regular. It looks like the hand of a literate person to me,' Bould said, studying it closely.

'Then the 'your' is most likely a blind, to confuse us.' He chewed some more. 'Unless he couldn't find the word he actually wanted in the paper and settled for this one on the basis that its meaning would be obvious. Now all we have to do is find out why someone wants to wipe out the whole Boot family. Here's what we'll do first. We'll pay a visit to William Boot; let's see if he's received one of these letters and perhaps we'd better find out if there are any other family members that we know nothing about. If there is someone out there intent on knocking them all off one by one, they will all need to be offered protection.' He picked up the phone and stabbed an extension number into it. Before it rang three times, someone at the other end answered. 'Aaron, get on the phone to Latham Hall and tell William Boot we're on our way to visit him.'

⋆　⋆　⋆

There were two large coaches in the car park and what seemed to Cobb like a thousand small children milling around.

It had rained overnight and although the sky was now clear, puddles had formed in a number of potholes in the gravel and the children were running around, screaming with delight and splashing through the water.

'Where are their teachers?' grumbled Cobb as he pushed through the pack and a small child careered into him. 'In my day we'd have been lined up in silence.'

The idea of his boss as a small child caused Bould to smile. 'They've been on the coach, so they're bound to want to let off steam.'

Making their way round the side of the house onto the long terrace, the full glory of the gardens hit them once again. The majestic sweep of the immaculately cut and rolled lawn running away to the marble fountain in the distance, with the water catching the light and breaking it up into a million dazzling diamonds, and just below the terrace, at their feet, the wide beds brimming over with flowers in hot colours. Even Cobb stood for a moment to enjoy the spectacle.

At the far end of the terrace another figure was similarly enjoying the view. It was William Boot. He had spotted the officers and now came towards them.

'Good morning, Inspector, Sergeant.' He indicated both with a sharp nod of his head. 'What can I do for you?'

Cobb produced the photocopy of the letter Adam had received. 'This came for your nephew this morning. I would be interested to know if you have received anything similar or if you are aware of your brother and sister-in-law getting such threats.'

'Your next,' Boot read out loud. 'I don't even know what that is supposed to mean. Your next what?'

'I would have thought it fairly explicit. His parents have both been murdered and this would suggest he will be the next victim. Now, we are still keeping an open mind as to why anyone would want to kill his parents — '

'What you mean is you haven't any leads,' Boot interjected bleakly.

'There is always the possibility that the killer intends to wipe out the whole family. That includes you, Mr Boot.' Watching for a reaction, Cobb was surprised to see Boot was dismissive of the danger.

'I doubt it. Why would anyone want to kill me?'

'Why would anyone want to kill your brother and his wife?'

A silence developed. Cobb and Boot locked gazes, but the man's face was as impassive as the policeman's.

In the end, it was Boot who looked away first. 'I have no idea, but then it's not my job to find out. I thought that was why we employed a police force.'

'Don't you want to see your brother and his wife's killer brought to justice? Most people do in your circumstances.' Bould spoke mildly, so his words hardly seemed reproachful.

In return he received a faintly contemptuous look. 'Of course I do, but I can't help you and frankly I would have thought you'd be better off doing some investigating instead of talking to me.' He paused before continuing in a more reasonable tone. 'I can assure you both that if I had received an anonymous letter of any description you'd be the first to know about it.'

'Very well.' It was the best he was going to get, although Cobb was far from happy with the man's attitude. 'Perhaps you can help us on another matter then. We have reason to believe a painting might have been taken from your brother's bedroom — possibly a Victorian depiction of Tewkesbury Abbey. Are you able to confirm that such a picture hung there?'

Boot blinked, and rubbed his eyes. 'Damn flies. I think one's just gone into my eye. It's those little black ones. We're plagued with them here at this time of year. We garden organically but there are times when I'd like to use pesticides — some pests need wiping out. It's a sad fact of life.' He blinked rapidly several times before answering Cobb's question. 'No, I can't tell you anything about it.

I've never been in my brother's bedroom. Why would I? We may have been close but we weren't that close. Although I have to tell you that Johnny was not particularly interested in paintings. It was Sylvia who liked to have them, not because she knew anything about art, you understand, but simply because she thought that's what people did — put chocolate-box daubs on their walls. She bought pictures simply to go with the room, rather than because she liked the artist or the subject matter.' During this conversation they had turned and began to slowly perambulate along the terrace.

'And you can never recall seeing one of Tewkesbury Abbey?' Cobb persisted. Just because the man had never been in the bedroom didn't mean he hadn't seen it. If Sylvia moved things around according to whim it could have been in another room at some time. Certainly, a search of the house had revealed no such painting to exist.

Boot's next words confirmed his suspicions. 'No, but that doesn't mean there wasn't one. Over the years, Sylvia bought many paintings, and after a time, when she was bored with them, they'd be disposed of and new ones purchased in their place.' They had to alter their path to avoid the massive, gnarled trunk of an ancient wisteria, and

Boot came to a halt, one hand on the tree. Turning to address Cobb, he said: 'Am I to understand that you think that this missing painting could have something to do with Johnny and Sylvia's death?'

'I don't know if it is connected or not, but it's a possibility we have to consider. All I'm trying to do, in the first instance, is establish exactly when the picture was removed. Mrs Boot could have taken it down herself, but equally the killer could have got into the house the day she died. Your nephew confirmed the French windows were open when he left, but as nothing else appears to be missing, I would like to trace it if I can.'

His words seemed to satisfy Boot, who nodded diffidently in reply, but made no comment.

Pressing on, Cobb returned to their earlier topic. 'As I've already said, we might be dealing with someone who wants to wipe out your entire family. This would suggest to me that there is someone out there with a grudge against the Boots. Can you think of anyone who would feel this way? The way I see it, to want to destroy an entire family suggests a very deep-seated sense of injustice. The motive may well be known to those family members still alive, so I'm asking you once more, Mr Boot, if you are aware of any such person.'

'And I can only repeat what I have already told you: I can think of no reason why anyone would want to kill either Johnny or Sylvia. They were well loved and well respected — haven't you read the press coverage?' Boot had moved away from the shade of the great wisteria to gaze out at the gardens beyond the balustrade, and his remarks were addressed more to the air than the officers.

'What about other members of your family?' Bould asked. 'We'd like to talk to them.'

'There aren't any.' Finally, something seemed to strike Boot. He recoiled as if dealt a slap in the face. 'There's just Adam and me left now.' A rather sad little sigh escaped from between set lips.

Cobb fished in his pocket and extracted a sheet. 'If you think of anything useful, Mr Boot, please contact me or one of my officers on any of these numbers. Night or day.'

On their return to the car park they found it deserted, the school children gone.

'I think we'll pay a visit to the council offices next; there's someone I want to talk to who seems to be the only level-headed person we've dealt with so far,' Cobb said as he climbed into the passenger seat.

Bould thought he could guess who this person was. 'Masie Hintlesham?'

'The one and only.'

'Probably just as well she's unique. I'm not sure the world's ready for too many like the new mayor.' Bould smiled as he opened the driver's door and climbed in.

Somehow Cobb's seatbelt had got twisted, and he didn't reply until it was sorted. 'No, I can't imagine tact appears too high on her list of qualities, but she's a straight talker and that's the sort I like. She'll run those council meetings without any nonsense, and I'll bet you a pound to a nine-bob note that she knows everything that goes on there.'

10

They found the mayor in her parlour, divesting herself of a heavy set of ceremonial robes.

'Good timing there,' Masie said, pulling the gold chain of office over her head. 'Been to some ghastly reception with the rest of the local chain gang. Only just got back.' On seeing their blank expressions, she clarified her words by waving the mayoral chain at them. 'Chain gang: other mayors or their deputies.' She threw herself down into one of several leather bucket seats ranged around a coffee table, and indicated the officers should do the same.

'You don't enjoy that sort of thing?' Bould hazarded a guess.

'Not a bit. I'm a doer, not a talker. So what can I do for you?'

Cobb took his time replying, and Masie misunderstood the pause.

'Sorry, where's m'manners? Would you care for a drink? Just help yourselves from the fridge.'

' 'We're fine, thank you.' Cobb declined for them both. 'When we met before you pointed us in the direction of Artemis Dukoy and I had a feeling that you might be just the person to talk to about a lot of things.'

She caught on in an instant. 'Did you indeed?' This amused her and she gave her alarming bark of a laugh. 'You're probably right. So, come on, who do you want me to dish the dirt on?' Bright eyed and eager, like a happy dog, she slapped her hands on her knees in expectation.

'Have you ever been in the Boots' house?'

'Only once. Think I made it plain before, I couldn't stand the man.'

'So you wouldn't know anything about any paintings he owned?'

'Paintings! The man was a complete Philistine, as was his wife. Money and social standing; those were the only things they cared about. Can't say I ever noticed any paintings particularly. Why d'you ask?'

'One appears to be missing from the house and we are interested to know if it is significant.'

'I bet you'd find plenty of people who would cheerfully have murdered the old bugger without needing the inducement of a painting,' Masie snorted.

'Nevertheless, we are keen to find out what has happened to this painting. It was of Tewkesbury Abbey.'

'Bet it was only a print. Boot was a man who, as they say, knew the price of everything and the value of nothing.'

'The actual value of the painting might not be relevant,' Bould said.

'Y'mean it could have some special significance to his killer?' In a little passageway linking the mayor's parlour to her working office was a galley kitchen and now Masie sprang from her seat and strode over to the area. She busied herself filling an electric kettle. 'If you don't fancy a beer, do you want to join me in a pot of tea?' she called.

'That would be most welcome,' Cobb replied. He enjoyed this woman's company. There probably weren't many Masie Hintleshams left any more. She was part of a dying breed: that formidable bunch of women who had carried the country along for centuries, doing their duty come hell or high water.

Masie reappeared with cups of fine porcelain bearing the gold crest of the council, and a packet of chocolate digestives. She offered them to Cobb with the true, but not particularly flattering, remark: 'You look like a man who enjoys a biscuit or two.'

As he was, he didn't refuse and neither did his sergeant.

Masie then put the packet on the little circular table around which they were gathered with the invitation: 'Help yourselves. Now, come on. Let's hear it. There's a missing painting and you think it might be why old Jack Boot was murdered, d'you?'

'We have no particular reason at the moment to link it to the deaths of Mr Boot or his wife, but we would like to account for it.'

'Wouldn't surprise me to learn he'd been caught out at last,' Masie said with some gravity.

'Meaning?' Cobb asked.

'There have been rumours about him for years. He's about as straight as a corkscrew but he's fly, I'll give him that. You'd never catch the blighter out. Perhaps you should be looking at all the folks he's done down over the years.'

'You're suggesting he was involved in some shady business deals?' Bould said, taking all this down in his ubiquitous notebook.

Masie suddenly seemed to remember the motto 'discretion is the better part of valour' and her position as mayor. 'Not for me to say, but you ask around. Start with that solicitor of his. Man's an out-and-out crook.' If she had made a resolution to be discreet it hadn't lasted long.

Cobb wondered if Masie know what discretion was. 'What about Quentin Make-peace?'

'What about him? You surely don't have him in mind as a killer. Have you met the man?' When the DI nodded in reply, Masie went on: 'I expect every council in the country has a Quentin Makepeace or two, usually retired folk with bugger all else to do. Some of the councillors find him tedious, but I rather think people like him are good for democracy. You can't put anything past Makepeace. He's got brains — which is more than I can say for some of my colleagues here.'

'But he was embroiled in a serious dispute with Mr Boot and his brother.'

Masie gave him a 'you cannot be serious' look that was almost comical. 'If you're referring to his assertion that he got his brother the job at Latham Hall, we *all* thought William Boot's appointment stank. Makepeace was the only one foolish enough to say it.'

'Why was that?' asked Bould, looking up.

'Because he can't be reported to the ombudsman.'

'You'll have to explain that,' Cobb said.

Helping herself to another biscuit, Masie waved it at them like an offensive weapon. 'It's the main hobby of half the councillors — reporting each other to the ombudsman. Y'see, the trick is to insult somebody heartily without naming them. You can say what you like: doesn't have to be true. In fact, the more lurid it is the better. However, if you're mad enough to name a councillor even if you're telling the truth, unless you can prove what you're saying he'll be straight to the ombudsman before you can blink.'

'And then what happens?'

'Depends.' She took a fearsome bite out of the biscuit and they waited whilst she chomped happily on it. 'You might just get a telling off, but you can be suspended or even barred from public office. Makepeace, being a member of the public, wouldn't be faced with that.'

'But he was being threatened with court action for libel from both the Boot brothers — that would have been considerably more damaging.'

'They'd never have seen him in court; they wouldn't have dared. It would have been far too risky.' A snort of derision accompanied her words. 'I don't know what William was up to but it was just old Jack Boot's way of having some fun. He hated Makepeace and enjoyed worrying the man the way a terrier worries a rat.'

'Did it work?'

'No idea. The only time I've ever seen Makepeace is when he comes to council meetings.'

'And does he do that a lot?'

'He's there for every meeting the public can attend.'

'But that must take up most of his time,' Bould interjected.

The mayor shrugged and helped herself to another biscuit. 'He's got nothing better to do.'

'To return to the matter of William Boot's appointment.' Cobb was keen to steer the conversation back to the matter in hand. 'Does this sort of thing go on much?'

'This sort of thing? You mean do councillors pull a fast one to get their relatives lucrative jobs? It used to happen all the time but I'm going back thirty, forty years. The muck's been shovelled out of the pig sty since then and it doesn't usually happen now. Good thing too.'

'So his appointment could have upset a lot of people.'

Masie considered this whilst absentmindedly nibbling on yet another biscuit. It was astonishing she was as thin as she was in view of the amount she ate. 'Not enough for anyone to kill him over it. If his shenanigans were enough to drive someone to murder, Boot would have been dead twenty years ago. All I can say over his brother's appointment is that the only folk who lost out were the other applicants for the job, and defeated candidates don't go around knocking off their rivals.'

'Still, I'd like to hear anything concrete you might know about his business dealings. You've hinted at certain things but that isn't enough for us to go on.'

'Sorry. Can't help you with details. I know bugger all about his business. All I can say is that he spent precious little time there. If you ask me, he wasn't much of a surveyor.'

'How do you know that?' Bould asked, curious.

'Because he was always hanging around the Council House — and if he wasn't there he was on holiday somewhere. Took a lot of holidays, did old Jack Boot, and he didn't believe in slumming it either.'

This wasn't much use to his investigation. Cobb tried once more, asking urgently this time. 'I really need something more specific.'

'As I say, the man was fly. I can't give you chapter and verse; it was just that everyone knew the man was rotten to the core. There were always stories doing the rounds about how he could be bought, but that's all I can give you — not enough, is it?' Once again, Cobb was struck by the shrewdness in the gaze she fixed him with.

They left Masie still munching her way

through the biscuits and headed for the lifts, but as Bould hit the call button Cobb hesitated.

'Whilst we're here, let's visit the personnel department and take a look at William Boot's CV. I'd like to see if there is any truth in the story that the late mayor got his brother the job.'

'But as Masie said, it's not much of a motive for murder,' Bould replied.

'No, but it might give us a better idea of the sort of man Boot was. All we've heard so far is nothing but idle speculation. We've heard allegations that Boot was corrupt, but where's the evidence? If we could at least nail this one on the head it will take us further in as much as we'll have a better grasp of the man's character.'

'Excuse me, could you tell us where to find your personnel department?' The lift had arrived, and Cobb took the opportunity to accost a young man alighting at their floor.

He looked baffled for a moment, and then the light dawned. 'Oh, you mean human resources — third floor.'

'Human resources!' Cobb exploded as the lift doors shut behind them. It was a pet gripe of his. Any organization that renamed its personnel department human resources was suspect in his view.

His prejudices were further confirmed when they arrived at the third floor and found the sprawling human resources offices.

'Yes. Can I help you?' A bored middle-aged woman looked up from her computer as they entered.

Having showed her his ID, Cobb asked to see the head of the department.

'Do you mean the director, the head of service, or a team leader?' his interlocutor asked.

He was getting too old for this game. It was the same everywhere. Too many chiefs and not enough Indians. 'Just find me the most senior person here,' he said curtly.

That turned out to be Penelope Golightly, who announced herself as director of human resources. As her hair and dress looked like she had just stepped out of the 1950s, Cobb was unsure as to whether this meant she was very fashionable or simply several decades behind the times. With her brunette hair swept up and pinned in a low bun, thick make-up and narrow, heavy-framed glasses which didn't detract from her bright blue eye shadow, she could have been any age between thirty and fifty.

'If this is confidential, as I'm sure it is, we'll go into my office. Do follow me.'

Her office was sterile and impersonal,

which seemed rather ironic given her job, and she seated herself behind her desk as if about to conduct a job interview with the officers.

Cobb came straight to the point. 'I'd like to see Mr William Boot's CV and job application for the post he holds at Latham Hall.'

With a rather sad little shake of her head and a beatific smile, Penelope said, 'I couldn't possibly allow that. It's confidential, you see.'

It was proving to be a long and difficult day, and Cobb could feel his temper waving him goodbye. 'Madam, we're conducting a murder enquiry. I'm afraid I don't give two hoots for your views on confidentiality. If necessary I'll get a search warrant and have the whole place turned upside-down, which will be guaranteed to get everyone in the building speculating on what's going on, so why don't you just give us the information we require and that way we can keep the matter between ourselves.'

Her eyes flickered uncertainly from Cobb to Bould and back as she considered her options. It didn't take Penelope long to reach a decision. 'I'm sure you will understand that my first consideration is, at all times, discretion.' She had one of those annoyingly soothing voices, as if she expected everyone she met to be angry and in need of calming down. 'In the normal scheme of things, I couldn't possibly allow you to see a confidential job application but given the circumstances, and your threat to obtain a search warrant, then I am prepared to allow my qualms to be set aside for the greater good.' She rose and left the room, which was probably just as well, given Cobb's mood.

'Greater good!' he said in a non-too-quiet voice to his sergeant. 'Who the hell does she think she is — Mother Teresa?'

It was some time before Penelope reappeared, clutching a yellow folder. 'Here we are,' she said in her soothing voice as she handed it over to the DI. 'I must ask you to look at it in this room. You cannot take it outside of here.'

'If I think it could be evidence I'll most certainly be taking it wherever I deem necessary.'

'How could it possibly be evidence?' She returned to her seat and Cobb realized she was one of those people who needed to hide behind a desk to feel powerful.

He didn't reply, but opened the file and located William Boot's CV. Bould moved closer so that he could read the document over his boss's shoulder.

'I assume you took up the references shown here?' the DI asked eventually.

'But of course we did, and let me say they were excellent.'

'That's as may be, but Mr Boot doesn't have a background in restoration of historical houses.'

'You will see, Inspector, that the job title is project manager. We were more concerned with an applicant's ability to attract funding for the project.'

'He doesn't seem to have a background in fundraising, either.' The CV was quite long, consisting of several pages stapled together, and Cobb quickly flicked through the lot. It struck him that the main achievement William Boot could claim was a propensity for blowing his own trumpet. The CV was full of the most extraordinary boasts. 'I'd like a copy of this.' He indicated the papers in his hand as he addressed Penelope.

She appeared dismayed. 'I've already told you, this file is confidential.'

'And I've already told you this is a murder investigation. Serious allegations have been made to me about how Mr Boot obtained his job, and I need to ascertain if they could have any bearing on his brother's death.'

She tried again, rallying herself valiantly, spreading her hands out, palms towards Cobb as if to physically ward him off. 'There was absolutely no impropriety about Mr

Boot's appointment. As I've said, we took up his references and they were exemplary, and he gave a splendid account of himself during the interview process.'

'In that case you've got nothing to worry about.' He continued holding out the file towards her and after a slight hesitation, Penelope took it.

'Wait here and I'll arrange to have this copied,' she said with ill grace, the softly soothing tone of her voice replaced by something altogether harder.

As the door closed behind her, Cobb turned to his sergeant. 'What did you think of it?'

'High on self-praise, low on substance. Do you want me to check out the references when we get back?'

'I do. He wouldn't be the first to supply false referees, and these days anyone can produce a convincing letterhead on their own computer.'

'But would it be a motive for murder?'

'Only for someone who was completely mad.' A heavy sigh of exasperation escaped the DI's lips. 'I know, we're probably barking up the wrong tree, but all the same, we will check out William's appointment.'

The door opened and Penelope returned with a sheaf of papers. 'Here you are. I hope you will use the utmost tact and discretion when contacting any organization mentioned. You will understand my first duty is to uphold the council's integrity at all times.'

Cobb never took kindly to being lectured in how to do his job. He took the papers without comment, other than to bid her a short goodbye.

As Bould drove them back to the station, Cobb preoccupied himself with reading Boot's job application and CV more thoroughly. He frowned once or twice and jotted down some questions in the margin, only looking up as the car turned into the station car park.

11

'At last. I wondered when you were going to come and see me.' Dr Bolton, the pathologist, managed to turn his remark into reproach.

It was nine o'clock the following day, and Cobb was finding it harder and harder to get on with the man, and wished yet again that Jenny had not retired. She was as warm and friendly as Bolton was cold and distant.

'I've not missed anything, I see,' Cobb responded, indicating the body of Sylvia Boot on the slab in the middle of the lab. 'And the traffic getting across town was abysmal. The hospital car park was full as well and I had the devil of a job finding a space.'

The PM was taking place, as always, in the basement of the town's General Hospital. Built in Victorian times, the General was pokey, dark and supremely depressing.

'Well, I've started. I delayed half an hour waiting for you.' The accusation was clear not just in the words but the icy glare that accompanied them.

'If you're running late you'd better get on with it then, hadn't you? Do you have anything of use to tell me yet?'

'She's been strangled — garrotted more like as I said before — with this piece of garden twine. Took me a devil of a time to remove it because it's cut deep into her flesh.' A bloody piece of string was held up in a pair of forceps for the DI's inspection. 'You see how long it is? The killer doubled it up six times to make it strong and thick enough to do the job.'

'The SOCO team found a ball of twine in the Boot's garden shed — can you say if it came from there?'

'You can buy this stuff anywhere.' Bolton shrugged as if to say that proved nothing.

Cobb persisted, considering that answer was of no use. He raised his voice. 'Can you not tell if it came from the ball we found at the Boots' house?'

'No. Only that it could have. But it could have come from one of a million like it. It's made by a factory that supplies the big DIY chains under generic names as well as under its own.'

'So the killer could have brought it with him as likely as not?'

A nod of confirmation. 'Yes.'

'Are we looking for a man, or could a woman have been responsible for this?'

Bolton indicated the victim's neck. 'I think it would be a man. There would need to be a lot of force used to kill her, and she wasn't a small woman. The killer stood behind her and looped the twine round her neck, so.' He sketched the air in demonstration. 'Then crossed the ends to get the necessary leverage.'

'Anything else to tell me?'

Bolton shook his head. 'No. She was in good health; there were no traces of drugs, alcohol or any untoward substances in her body as far as I can tell, although I have sent tissue samples off to toxicology.'

With the PM over, Cobb left the lab with a sense of despondency that he knew was irrational. What had he been expecting the pathologist to tell him? It was the garden twine that depressed him. It could have come from anywhere. As at this precise moment, he had nothing to go on at all. Two murders in just over a week and no leads. It was time to cast the net wider.

Back at the station he found Bould in the CID room poring over the data that Ian Constable had turned up on Boot's finances.

'Anything of use to us?' It was a question asked more in hope than expectation.

'Doesn't appear to be. The money that came into Boot's bank every month as interest from his deposit accounts seems legit in as much as he's had these deposits for over twenty years. They were originally opened with substantial amounts but after all this time it's going to be next to impossible to find out where he got the money from.'

'Great.' Cobb felt his mood get gloomier by the minute. 'Leave that for now. I think we should talk to Councillor Dukoy's husband. She might very well claim that her husband didn't mind her having an affair with Boot, but let's hear it from his own lips.'

'Do you think he might have killed Boot out of jealousy? But if he did, why would he kill Sylvia?' Bould shuffled the wad of papers together and tapped them on the desk to square them into a neat pile, which he then placed into an orange folder.

'Don't. I know. Whatever theory we come up with for Boot's death we just hit a brick wall when we try to work out how his wife's murder fits into things. So, let's just go and talk to the man — see what that turns up.'

Dukoy Holdings was based in an elegant Regency townhouse in the elegant Regency town of Cheltenham Spa. Only a small brass plate to the side of the dark blue door gave any intimation that this was not a private residence.

An entryphone system screened visitors and their press on the bell was answered by an efficient young woman who sounded as if she had been educated at the nearby Ladies College.

They found themselves let into a narrow hall with a thick cream carpet underfoot, an octagonal table under a large gilt mirror and a couple of paintings on the walls that surprised them. For whilst everything else was redolent of the early eighteenth century, the paintings were bold, modern abstracts. The one opposite the mirror was a splodge of crimson across a white background. Out of the corner of his eye, Cobb realized it was possible to make out two faces in the swirling red yet when he turned head on to look squarely at it, the faces disappeared and only a mess of paint confronted him.

The other painting was of an overlapping set of rectangles in varying shades of blue, again on a white background.

'These are original Betinskis,' Bould said, sounding impressed.

'Never heard of him,' his boss replied.

'Her. Aurora Betinski. These would be worth a couple of hundred thousand each.' Standing in front of the blue rectangles, Bould was enraptured.

'People must have more money than sense. If I had that amount spare I'd — '

But before the DI could give full vent to his views on modern art, the door to the front reception room opened and a young woman came forward, her hand outstretched, a welcoming smile sketched on her exquisitely made-up face. 'Hello, how do you do? I'm Alison Spencer, Mr Dukoy's personal assistant. Please do follow me.' After the most perfunctory of handshakes, Alison set off up the stairs and the officers followed in her wake.

She went at a queenly pace, giving Cobb plenty of time to appraise her. The first thing that struck him was that, for entirely different reasons, Alison had been picked for the image she portrayed just as much as the solicitor Bartley's PA. But Alison was the antithesis of the half-witted Marilyn. Tall and willowy, with dark hair swept up high on her head and held in place with what looked like two knitting needles to Cobb, Alison wore a green dress that hugged her figure. Her stiletto-heeled shoes were the same colour as the dress, and looked about as expensive.

At the top of the stairs, she halted, tapped gently on an unmarked door, and in response to a murmur from within, ushered Cobb and Bould forward.

The room they found themselves in was so brilliant with sunshine pouring in through wall-to-ceiling windows that Gregory Dukoy was just a dark silhouette as he rose from behind his writing table.

'Good morning, gentlemen.' With a slight inclination of his head, Dukoy acknowledged his visitors. Then he turned and indicated the view from the window. 'I never tire of telling myself how lucky I am to be working here.'

From his tone and the way he stepped aside, they understood it was required of them to admire the view and so they moved closer. Beneath them was the private garden of the house. Their gazes fell on a stripped lawn beringed with beds full of old-fashioned plants in muted colours that fitted perfectly with the age of the house. High stone walls surrounded this fertile oasis, screening out the rest of the world.

'I'm not surprised,' Bould said.

'Very nice,' the DI concurred, although he had only given the scene a cursory glance. 'Do you have any deadly nightshade growing down there?'

'What a most peculiar question. Of course I don't. It's an extremely poisonous plant — why on earth would I want to grow such a thing?'

'Why indeed?' Cobb was at his most bland. 'Now, Mr Dukoy, we want to speak to you about the death of Mr Jonathan Boot.'

'Whilst I'm more than happy to help you in any way I can, I don't see what possible use to your investigation I can be.'

'We'll be the judge of that,' Cobb said pleasantly enough, but Bould recognized the slight edge that told him his boss didn't take kindly to a potential witness, or suspect, in a murder investigation taking a negative attitude from the word go.

Now they had the light behind them, the officers could see that Gregory Dukoy was a big man who was a lot older than his wife. His skin was deeply tanned and his grey, grizzled hair thinning. At first glance he appeared to be well fleshed out, but as he turned, the light cast shadows into hollow cheeks and his hand-stitched suit hung looser than it should. It looked as if he had lost a lot of weight in a very short space of time. His look was studiously casual chic, very expensive casual chic: a linen suit in soft, smudgy grey over a steel-grey shirt, open neck, no tie.

At this point, the DI hesitated, knowing that he might be about to hit Dukoy with a bombshell. It was all very well Artemis insisting she and her husband had an open marriage and both had affairs, but he was also well aware that many people lied to the police, particularly if they were likely to be a prime suspect in a serious crime case. 'Have you and your wife been married long?' This was a neutral remark and he could be guided by Dukoy's response.

'Oh, yes, Inspector. We've been married twenty years and it doesn't seem like a day under fifty.'

Good. This was just the opening he had hoped for. It would appear Artemis hadn't been lying.

'You and Mrs Dukoy don't get on, then?' Bould asked, with just a hint of irony.

Instead of replying, Dukoy stared long and hard out of the window. He was thinking, and when he had marshalled his thoughts he turned back to the officers. 'My wife and I have different tastes.' It was delicately put.

'Meaning?' Cobb thought he got the drift but needed it spelt out.

Raising his head, Dukoy turned the full blast of an intense gaze at the DI. 'I'm not terribly interested in women, if you understand me.'

'In that case, I feel obliged to ask why you married Mrs Dukoy.'

A rather superior smile flitted across Dukoy's face. 'I fear you're being rather naïve, now, Inspector. There are many reasons to marry apart from love. In business, for instance, it's important to be able to have a wife to take to functions, or for when I need to entertain business clients at home. Artemis understood the situation before we married,

128

so my conscience is clear. We both got what we wanted out of the deal.'

'Really? What was in it for Mrs Dukoy?'

'Artemis had a lifestyle and standing in the community she wouldn't otherwise have had. She's a very high-maintenance woman, in case you hadn't realized. As long as she was there to appear on my arm when necessary, she had a blank cheque book and the freedom to amuse herself in whatever way she chose.'

'So, can I take it that you knew about her and Jonathan Boot?'

'You can. Oh dear — there goes my motive. If you thought this was a classic case of a cuckolded husband, you've picked the wrong man.' He was laughing at them.

'What exactly is your business, Mr Dukoy?' Cobb switched subject effortlessly.

'I'm a property developer.'

Out of the corner of his eye, Cobb saw his sergeant's head come up.

'In this area?' Bould asked.

'In any area there's money to be made. South and west Gloucestershire mainly, but throughout the Cotswolds too. Lots of money around there.'

'So you must have come across Jonathan Boot in his capacity as chair of the planning committee.' The words were spoken quietly, but Dukoy understood the implication behind the DI's words instantly.

'I come across all the chairs of all the relevant councils' planning committees and all their planning officers on a routine basis, Inspector. And I'm squeaky clean. The days when you could bribe planners have long gone. I think you'll find John Poulson sounded that particular death knell. Wasn't it of him that Edward Heath made his famous remark about the unacceptable face of capitalism?'

There was something totally insincere about Dukoy. Cobb could sense the man laughing up his sleeve at him, and he didn't believe a word of what he had just said — apart from the remark about Poulson, which he did vaguely remember. But two could play at that game, and he replied smoothly: 'No one has said anything about bribes but I am interested in the fact that that was the first thing you thought of. I simply meant you must have known Mr Boot, even if it was only professionally.' He had the satisfaction of seeing how uneasy he had made Dukoy.

Regret showed briefly in the other man's eyes but he turned away with a shrug and occupied himself by studying his garden once more. 'Yes, of course I knew Councillor Boot but, as you say, only professionally. Some of my developments were so big they had to be called in to the planning committee and then I would personally address those committee members present as, I may say, would any objectors to my scheme and what's more any member of the public can attend these meetings. They are entirely open and above board.'

'Have you ever come across a Quentin Makepeace?' Cobb didn't need an answer — he saw it in the sudden tension in Dukoy's shoulders.

Then the man relaxed and fixed a bland smile to his face and turning, 'No, I've never heard of him.'

He was lying, Cobb was convinced of it, but there was no way he could prove it, so he contended himself by saying, 'One final question: can you think of any reason why someone would kill Mr and Mrs Boot?'

'Indeed I cannot. As I said, I only knew him professionally and her not at all.'

It was only what he had expected but Cobb still felt a strong sense of frustration. The man didn't care, wasn't interested, wouldn't help them even if he could, and that sudden last realization was very forceful. 'Well, thank you for your time, Mr Dukoy. If you think of anything helpful to our enquiry, please contact me or my team on these numbers.' Cobb handed over the list of contacts but had a feeling it would go straight in the bin the moment they left the room.

As they descended the stairs, the front door opened and a man came in. He seemed as surprised to see them as they did him.

Cobb spoke first. 'Well, well, Mr Bartley, fancy seeing you here.'

Bartley recovered quickly, smiled the smile a shark might manage, and said: 'Why? You must have a strange view of solicitors if you think they only have one client.'

'So Mr Dukoy is a client of yours, is he?' Bould asked.

'His company is — Dukoy Holdings. I specialize in commercial firms and planning law.'

Before the officers could speak further, the door to Alison's office opened and she stepped into the space between the three men. 'Good morning, David. I'll take you straight up.'

It didn't escape either policeman that she had pinked slightly as she spoke and subconsciously smoothed her dress.

As soon as Bould had turned the car out of the tiny car park that had been created from the front garden, his boss started voicing his thoughts.

'There's a connection here that needs investigating. Bartley was Boot's solicitor and he's also Dukoy's. Boot was having an affair with Dukoy's wife. We've only his word for it that he didn't mind. Boot was chair of planning and Dukoy is a property developer. And he said he didn't know Makepeace, but I think he's lying.'

'You think this is about corruption?' Bould braked sharply as a youth on a pedal cycle shot without warning across the road. 'Sorry, sir,' he apologized as both officers were thrown forward.

'Not your fault. Some youngsters seem to have a death wish. We'll get Ian to check out the financial affairs of Dukoy Holdings and David Bartley's firm. I don't trust either of those two, and it's too much of a coincidence. And then there's Adam Boot — he inherits a lot of money. People have been killed for considerably less than two million pounds. I think we need to look closely at his finances as well. Let's see just how healthy his web design business is.'

12

When they returned to the station, Cobb went straight to the CID room. It was deserted apart from Rose, who was at her desk engaged in writing up some notes.

'Any luck in discovering what Boot had to eat and drink the day he died?' the DI asked.

Looking up, Rose replied, 'I'm just writing my report now, sir.'

'Good. What did you find out.'

'On the morning of his death he was opening the Stephen Street Community Centre in Mallerton. There was some light refreshment afterwards: just a finger buffet and orange juice or tea and coffee. There were a lot of people present but I don't see how anyone could have tampered with his food without risking poisoning a lot of other people at the same time.'

'Can we get a list of all those who attended?'

She looked doubtful. 'I can try but it wasn't strictly invitation only. The doors were open to all: it is part of their motto 'our doors are always open' and they take it literally so any member of the public could walk in.'

Drawing on his own experience in attending community events, Cobb said: 'I shouldn't imagine many people other than those with a vested interest in the centre attended, which means those who were invited will have been in the majority, so a guest list will be helpful.'

'I'll get on to it right away, sir.'

'OK. Next question: did Boot get his own food from the finger buffet or did someone plate it up for him?'

'The mayor got his own. He liked to be treated just like everyone else, they say.'

'Hmmm. I think that depends on who you speak to.'

'John Carrington — he's a council officer — was there in his role of head of community services, and he told me he offered to get the mayor something to eat, as Mr Boot was talking to a woman called.' Here Rose broke off to consult her handwritten notes. She flicked back a couple of pages until she found what she was looking for. 'Joan Cashmore.'

'And she is . . . ?'

'Chair of the community centre's management committee. She's not employed by the council: the management committee is made up of volunteers who live in the area. Well, Mr Carrington offered to get some food for them both but the mayor insisted on getting his own. Not that there was much. It was just after 11.30 and there were only a few sandwiches, sausage rolls and small cakes on offer, but apparently there was still quite a crush of people around the buffet table with everyone helping themselves at random.'

'Right. In that case I think we can rule out the possibility of atropine being added to the food at this do as there would be no way our killer could be certain of hitting his target. What about drink?'

'He had a cup of tea which he fetched himself.'

'Did someone pour the tea out for him, though?' The timing pointed to the community centre being the right place, so Cobb pursued the issue doggedly. If it wasn't the food, it had to be the tea.

'Yes, one of the helpers. A Claire Trowle, but everyone who had tea had it poured from the same pot, and the same goes for the milk — it was in a jug on the table and there was just the one bowl of sugar.'

'What about later? Was that all he had to eat and drink before he died?'

'No, sir, after this he came back to the council offices for the council meeting, but before it started he went to the canteen and got himself something to eat.'

'What time would this have been?'

Again Rose consulted her notes. 'Just after one, sir.'

'Hmm. If Bolton is to be believed that would have been too late. What did he have?'

'Curry, sir. Plated up by a canteen assistant called Ella Williams, and ladled out of the usual metal containers.'

'So the poison, if it had been added there, would have to have been put into the mayor's own plate after it had been dished up. Was the mayor alone?'

'Yes, sir.'

The more Cobb fired questions at Rose, the faster she responded and all the time he became more and more frustrated with the answers. Not that he blamed Rose, or found her wanting in any way, it was just the fact that someone had poisoned Boot and yet there seemed to be no way it could have been done. He asked one last question of her. 'For the sake of completeness, what did he have to drink in the canteen?'

'Water, sir. Poured from a communal water cooler.'

'Hmm.' They seemed to be banging their heads on a brick wall. Cobb changed the subject. 'Do you know where my sergeant is? I need a word with him.'

'He and Aaron have gone to Warwick, sir.

He said there was something they needed to check out.'

★ ★ ★

Because it wasn't market day, the market square was jam packed with cars.

'Blast, I usually park here without problem,' Aaron said, but then on consideration added, 'but then I usually only come here in the evenings.'

'Bit far for a night out, I'd have thought,' Bould remarked.

'I used to go out with a girl from these parts. There used to be a great little wine bar just south of the square. Mind you, I'm going back a bit. I think I'd better try the multi storey.' Aaron gave up cruising for a space and swung his car round a dog leg formed by a corner of the solid bulk of the county museum — a Victorian addition that narrowed the square at one end — before heading towards an incongruous concrete car park towering above the rooftops of the medieval buildings that still formed the heart of this historic town.

The car park was all but empty and they were able to get a space on the ground floor. As Bould unfolded himself from the passenger seat he said: 'If you know the town I take

138

it you know where Cocksparrow Street is.'

'Sorry sir. Never heard of it.'

'Just as well I printed a map off from the internet then,' Bould replied dryly and opened a single sheet of paper. 'It loops round to connect Linen Street and Theatre Street — ring any bells?'

'Oh, yes. I do vaguely remember Theatre Street. Can I see the map, sir?' A quick glance was all it took. 'Right, sir, I've got my bearings. It's this way.'

A five-minute walk took them to the narrow, meandering Cocksparrow Street. They were looking for number 45 and were expecting to find a private house belonging to a Lord Ragsdale. Or they would have been if Bould hadn't already found out that no such person owned a house in Warwick.

What they found instead was an old property converted into tiny offices. A little sign in the window read 'Wareham Services Ltd'.

'Well, let's see what we find in here, then,' said Bould as he pushed the door open.

They found themselves in what had once been a small living room. The fireplace was still there, together with a couple of desks. The back wall was covered in wooden pigeonholes, and a further wall was lined with a bank of filing cabinets.

Two men in their early thirties broke off from their conversation and turned to face the newcomers. Both were casually dressed in jeans and T-shirts, allowing the officers the chance to admire the tattoos covering their well-muscled arms.

'Yeah?' said the shorter one. 'Can I do something for you?'

Both policemen produced their ID.

'DS Bould and DC Price,' Bould said by way of introduction. 'And you are . . . ?'

'Frankie Snell, that's me, and my business partner here is Tony Coombs. Like I said, what can I do for you?'

'How long has your company had these offices?' Bould could see very little evidence of any work being undertaken.

'Ten years now.' Frankie appeared to be the spokesman for the company.

'Ten years.' The time was important. 'And what business is it that you conduct here?' The pigeonholes at the back were all marked with names, of both individuals and compa-nies, so Bould had already formed a very good idea of what Wareham Services offered.

Frankie's next words confirmed his suspi-cions. 'We're a mail collection and forwarding company.'

'You provide a poste restante address for people in return for a fee.' It wasn't a question but he got an answer anyway.

'Yeah, that's right. There's nothing illegal about it. If there are some as who don't want other people to know where they operate from, that's their business.'

Bould now knew for sure that William Boot had falsified his CV. Mallerton Council had offered him the job at Latham Hall after receiving a glowing reference from his last employer — a certain Lord Ragsdale of 45 Cocksparrow Street, Warwick. 'I'd like you to check your records. About three and a half to four years ago. I want to know if anyone by the name of Boot or Ragsdale used your services.'

Frankie looked shifty but he spoke confidently enough. 'No can do. We don't keep records that far back.'

'It must be in your books. You do keep proper accounts, I trust.'

The almost imperceptible look Frankie and his business partner exchanged was answer enough.

'Some people pay cash up front,' Tony said. He had been lounging against a desk, but now he stood up and they saw he was very tall and very fit.

'You still have to keep records,' Aaron said. He hadn't been taking notes up to then as they had no reason to believe it was necessary, but he now made a big show of getting his notebook out and stood, pen in hand, posed to write, hoping to unnerve the businessmen.

He succeeded. Tony looked uncertain, hesitated a moment and then started rummaging in a filing cabinet.

'It's a confidential service we offer,' Frank whined, trying to sound placatory.

'Sorry, there's nothing here. I thought there was but I was wrong. We've got rid of our records from that far back, and once we've filed accounts we move on. No point thinking about the past. We concentrate on the future.' Tony slammed the drawer shut.

It probably didn't matter; they were only here to tidy up some loose ends which may not have any bearing on their murder investigation, but Bould tried one last time. 'Have you ever heard of a Lord Ragsdale, or had any business dealings with him?'

'No and no. Sorry we can't help you, gentlemen.' Frankie smiled, showing a gold tooth.

★　★　★

On their return to the office Bould left Aaron to trace Lord Ragsdale if he could and went to find his superior.

Cobb was in his office, ploughing through a mountain of paperwork. He listened in silence until his sergeant had updated him on the morning's work. 'Good work, but I'm not sure how this fits in with the deaths of Mr and Mrs Boot so I don't want you to waste too much time on what might be a red herring. The fact that Boot's a liar and a cheat doesn't make him a murderer. Let Price talk to Ragsdale if he can trace him — if he exists even — and then we'll have a team meeting. There's one or two things we need to go through.'

It had turned 6.30 before Cobb was able to gather all four members of his team in the CID room.

He started by filling them in on what Rose had discovered.

'The murderer must have been present at the community centre opening,' Cobb ended by saying. 'That represents the only opportunity anyone had to administer the poison at the right time, although how they did it remains to be discovered. Rose is going to obtain a guest list and then we'll interview everyone present.'

'What about those not on the guest list, sir?' Ian said. 'The members of the public.'

'Whoever killed Boot had to know him. The only members of the public likely to be

143

present would be those who lived in the vicinity of Stephen Street. Rose, once you've got the guest list for the opening check out the electoral roll for the vicinity, see if there are any names there that jump out at you. Then get William Boot to have a look, see if he recognizes any. We might have to conduct house-to-house enquiries in the area as well, but we'll leave that for the moment.

'Aaron, did you manage to speak to Lord Ragsdale?'

'I did. He lives in Yorkshire, in a vast pile called Ragsdale Castle, but it's not a real castle, just a big house built by a Victorian mill owner who made a lot of money and wanted to join the upper classes. A previous Lord Ragsdale threw it open to the public in a bid to help with running costs. Boot claimed he worked there as the manager but his lordship tells me he's never heard of William Boot, he doesn't employ anyone to manage his property and he's never lived in Warwick.

'So how come the council didn't find this out?' Rose wondered. 'They said they took his references up.'

'I think Sergeant Bould can answer that one,' Cobb said and turned to his DS.

Bould summarized his morning's work.

'So, it would appear that Quentin Make-peace was right to believe there was something fishy going on,' Ian said.

'As Boot and his brother worked that very cleverly, how did Quentin Makepeace get the idea that something untoward was going on?' Rose asked.

'He was very vague when the boss and I saw him,' Bould said, turning to address the rest of the team. 'He was keen to assert that there was wrongdoing in the appointment but couldn't or wouldn't say how he knew.'

'That's right,' the DI confirmed. 'He was long on accusations and short on facts. So, the point I make is this: does he really know anything and if he does how did he come by his information?'

'Why did Boot want the job at Latham Hall so much that he was prepared to falsify his CV?' Rose asked. 'After all, if he'd been caught out he could have ended up in court. At the very least, he'd have had trouble getting another job.'

'Could this have something to do with the missing art collection?' Bould asked.

'In what way?' Cobb asked.

'No one knows what happened to the paintings. Perhaps Boot thinks they are hidden away somewhere in the hall and he might be able to find them. After all, he must have constant access to the house and presumably to the Latham family papers as well.'

Cobb scratched the back of his head. As an idea it had some merit. 'It's something we might look at but I think we ought to assume that whoever copied the paintings also spirited the originals away at the time. After all, it's over twenty-five years since the deception was uncovered. Nevertheless, I think we need to look into William Boot's background. Neil, run a check through the police computer and see if the man's got form. Unless he has I don't think we should read too much into his desire to work at Latham Hall. He might simply have been attracted by the salary. He wouldn't be the first person to be caught out lying on his CV in order to get a job.

'Aaron, do some discreet digging around, see what you can find out about Adam Boot. He's a website designer with his own company. I want to know how his finances stand and if he's living within his means, or whether his inheritance has arrived not a moment too soon.'

13

It hadn't rained for over a week and the few plants in Makepeace's garden were looking very sorry for themselves, but as Cobb and Bould walked up the drive of number 48 Poppyfield Crescent, the man himself appeared carrying a large watering can. He seemed less than pleased to see the officers.

'What do you want now?' he asked with a weary sigh.

'We've just got one or two further questions we'd like to ask you,' the DI replied in a sunny voice.

'Oh, very well, if you must.' The watering can was dropped with a thump on the driveway, slopping water everywhere.

Never having met a missionary before, Cobb wasn't sure what sort of personality was needed for the job, but whatever it was he didn't think Makepeace possessed it.

His sergeant obviously felt the same way, for as they followed Makepeace into the house Bould muttered, 'He seems rather short of the milk of human kindness.'

They were led back into the same room they had interviewed him in before.

'Well — how can I help you?' Makepeace stopped in the middle of the room and turned to face the officers with a grudging attempt at civility.

'It's to do with Mr William Boot's appointment at Latham Hall. You were very keen to accuse him of getting the job by undue influence or false pretences but can you explain to us why you think this to be the case?' Cobb said.

In an instant the man's whole demeanour changed. He was now very animated and profusely hospitable. 'A-ha! So you are going to take my complaint seriously. At last. I can't tell you what music this is to my ears. I've waited years for someone to listen to me. Sit down, why don't you? Can I get you something to drink? Tea, coffee, beer or whisky?'

'No, thank you, sir,' Cobb spoke for both of them. 'Not whilst we're on duty.'

'No? Oh well.' For a moment Makepeace seemed disappointed, but then he dismissed the matter with a shrug of his shoulders.

'Now, sir,' Cobb began, 'will you please tell us why you thought there was something suspicious about Mr Boot's appointment as project manager? I take it you have no real evidence or you would have handed this over to the relevant authorities.'

'Do you mean the council or the police? Because I have found neither to be interested in my concerns in the past. In my experience the only way to get something done is to do it yourself.' Almost immediately, Makepeace had reverted to his normal self and become truculent again.

The hackles rose on the back of Cobb's neck, as they always did when someone implied his force weren't doing their job, but he kept his voice sweet. 'Did you have any evidence to take to either body?'

It was obvious he had hit home with his arrow but Makepeace wasn't going to admit it and the man obfuscated as on their previous visit. 'You shouldn't need evidence if it's obvious something underhand is going on.'

'On the contrary, sir, evidence is exactly what you have to have if you want to make your case stick. So I ask again, why did you think there was something wrong with the appointment?'

'I've been up to Latham Hall — the gardens are open to the public but Boot is usually to be found loitering doing nothing despite being paid vast sums of rate payers' money. I've engaged him in conversation once or twice and it was clear to me he didn't know what he was talking about.'

'Do you know anything about restoring houses? I thought you'd been a missionary,' Bould said.

Makepeace looked as if he was about to explode. 'That doesn't preclude me from knowing about other things in life. As it happens, I have a great love for, and interest in, the architecture of Britain and that includes its stately homes. And yet, despite the fact that I have only a passing knowledge of such things, I am still of the opinion I know more than that jackass.' He looked dissatisfied with his own answer. 'It's like everything: you don't tend to notice how important something is in your life until it's not there. All around us in Britain we're exposed daily to our heritage, particularly our wonderful old buildings. Kenya has a long cultural history but it is very different to here as they have very few ancient monuments or buildings. When I retired and came back home, I found I had the time to indulge my passion for the past.'

'What church are you with?' Cobb asked.

'The Anglican, not that I see what it's got to do with your enquiries.'

'It's just personal curiosity. I didn't realize the Anglican Church still sent missionaries abroad. I thought that practice died with the Empire.'

'We do more than just convert people, you know. We set up schools, health centres, hospitals even. Our doctrine is to bring succour to the needy.'

'I had cause to visit Kenya some years ago. The poverty in the slums around Nairobi was shocking,' Bould said conversationally.

'I was up country, in villages in the Serengeti National Park. The people up there are poor, but the poverty is not so dreadful as it is in the cities. Their lives are hard and what they have is very basic but the squalor and disease that is rampant in the Nairobi slums are missing.' As Makepeace warmed to his theme, he grew passionate. It was obvious he cared deeply about what he was saying. 'Access to clean drinking water is probably the greatest threat they face on a daily basis. Many of these poor people have to trudge for two hours a day under a baking sun just to fetch water from a safe drinking source. Often it's the children who have to do this, and then they miss school and so their poverty is never-ending. We did a lot of work sinking boreholes within the village location to alleviate this.'

'Really? That's very interesting,' Bould said, and he did indeed sound interested.

His boss was becoming impatient. 'So your belief that William Boot wrongly got his job at

Latham Hall is down solely to your personal impression that he did not know as much as you about historic buildings and their restoration. Is that right?'

'Put like that, you make me sound opinionated and pompous,' Makepeace complained.

'As I've already stated, Mr Makepeace, unless you have evidence you can hardly be surprised that you were not taken seriously,' the DI replied wearily.

'And how am I, as a member of the public, supposed to come by this evidence? It is the people in authority who can do this. Do I assume that you have found some evidence now?'

'We'll ask the questions, if you don't mind, and we are only interested to know if you have any hard and fast reason to suspect Mr Boot's appointment as suspect. It would appear you haven't so we won't take up any more of your time. Good day to you, Mr Makepeace.'

14

A gravel path of honey-coloured Cotswold limestone led the mourners from the lych gate to the church porch. It was almost impossibly idyllic. The graveyard was compact, squeezed in between lush fields and a moated medieval farmhouse.

Cobb and Bould stood back from the assembled throng, standing in the shade of a tall yew tree. There weren't as many mourners as they had expected. Adam had asked that this double funeral be a private service and apart from him and his uncle there were few others in attendance. The officers recognized some as councillors, but noted more stayed away than felt the need to pay their respects.

As the bell ceased striking its single, mournful note and the last of the crowd made their way into the dark interior, Cobb and Bould followed in their wake.

After the short service, they were back outside once more, gathered around the grave. Cobb always found burials intensely moving and sad affairs in a way that cremations never were, and he was glad when it was over.

153

'You'll come up to the house, I hope,' Adam said as they prepared to take their farewells. 'I want my parents to have a decent send-off.'

As Cobb started to make an excuse, Adam went on: 'Actually, I'd really appreciate it. I don't feel very safe down here any more.' He spoke lightly, as if trying to make a joke out of it but couldn't hide his nervousness for all that.

'Have you had any more letters?' Bould asked.

'No. But then I'm working on the basis that whoever killed my parents doesn't know my London address, whereas they might not find it too difficult to discover the funeral's today and that I'd be down here. I'm not staying overnight. I'll go back to London this evening.'

'What are you going to do with the house now?' Cobb said.

'Sell it.' No hesitation there. 'I'm not a country lover. My life's in London these days and there is nothing here that would ever bring me back.'

They were walking slowly, as the occasion dictated, and arrived at the pocket handkerchief car park to find everyone else had already left, apart from one very elderly gentleman who stood by an old and battered

Rover as he fumbled for his car keys. He glanced towards them.

'Hello, I'm Adam Boot, and I don't think we've met before,' Adam said, approaching with his hand outstretched.

'Adam.' The old man appraised him with a shrewd eye. 'You must be Jonathan's son.'

'That's right, and you are . . . ?'

'Henry Winterbottom. I was your father's tutor when he was at university in London.'

'Good Lord! And you've come all this way, after all this time.' Adam seemed more than surprised; the expression writ large on his face was one of utter astonishment. 'How did you know about the funeral?'

'Your parents' deaths have been in all the papers,' Dr Winterbottom reminded Adam, but gently. His manner was one of decorous dignity and a charming sympathy seemed to envelop him like a cloak. 'It wasn't hard for an old codger like me to find out where and when the funeral would take place. I hope you don't mind me coming.'

'Not at all, and I do hope you'll come back to the house for some refreshment.'

Waving away Dr Winterbottom's protestations, Adam proceeded to give him detailed instructions as to the location of Foinavon, and it escaped neither Cobb's nor Bould's attention that the mention of the name of the

155

property seemed to strike a chord with the old man as he smiled and nodded to himself.

'I think we'll have a chat with the good doctor when we get to the house,' Cobb told his sergeant as they set off.

'Surely he can't have anything to do with our investigations — it's going to be decades since he last saw Boot. Or are you hoping for a fresh insight into the victim's character?' Bould let Dr Winterbottom go before him in order to make sure he kept on the right road.

'He'll give us a different perspective because no one else we've spoken to seems to have known Boot in his youth. I'd also like to know why Winterbottom has made the journey at his age. I can't believe he makes a habit of attending the funerals of all his past students, so what's this about?'

'Perhaps he's just ghoulish; attracted here because the Boots were murdered. There are some people like that.'

'Yes, the sort who attended public executions, but he didn't strike me as being that type of person. The ghouls are always eager to hear all the gory details — they're shameless in their desire to find out just how bloody the murders were. He struck me as a very thoughtful type.'

'Well, we'll soon find out.' Bould swung the car through ninety degrees and gravel crunched under the tyres as they drove slowly up the drive. 'Don't know where we're going to park, sir.'

'Just abandon it here then,' was the instruction from his boss. 'If anyone wants to go before us, they've only got to say.'

The French windows were open and the mourners had spilled out onto the lawn, standing together in a huddle, their dark clothing and subdued talk giving the effect of a garden party gone badly wrong.

The only guest who chose not to go outside was Dr Winterbottom, who had carefully lowered himself into the most comfortable and well-cushioned chair in the lounge and was busy tucking in to a full plate of finger food brought to him by Adam, who swiftly crossed the room to intercept the officers halfway.

'Gentlemen, there's plenty of food and drink in the dining room. Please feel free to help yourselves.'

That was a very tempting offer to Cobb but he ignored the rumbling of his stomach. 'Maybe later, Mr Boot. First I'd like to speak with Dr Winterbottom.'

Adam looked as if he would like to argue the finer points of the police using his parents' funeral to interrogate a mourner, but he swiftly removed the mutinous expression from his face and adopted a neutral tone. 'I hope you'll go gently with him. He's had a long journey to get here and seems rather frail to me. As a guest in my house I feel I have a duty to look after him.'

'Don't worry, sir. We don't want to upset him either,' Cobb replied in a tone that made it clear he knew best. 'Did your father ever mention Dr Winterbottom to you?'

'No, never. I didn't know he existed before today.'

'But you did know your father went to university in London?'

'No. I had no idea about that either. But then, that doesn't really surprise me. My parents never discussed their early lives with me. We all lived in the here and now. My mother used to say the past wasn't important, and I tend to agree with her.'

Cobb found this claim rather surprising. Most people are curious as to how their parents met, if nothing else. Still, he'd leave that one for the moment. 'Right, well, we'll just go and speak to Dr Winterbottom now, sir.' He dismissed Adam with a polite smile.

The old man was delicately picking at his food when they went through, and he happily put his plate to one side to talk. 'Jonathan was one of the best students I have ever seen. It was a crying shame he never pursued the career he was made for,' he began.

'And that would be?' Cobb prompted.

'Fine art,' Winterbottom said, and noticed the look that passed between the officers.

'But he was a quantity surveyor,' Bould said.

'Yes, that's what he trained as originally, apparently just to please his parents. His heart was never in it and he came to London as a mature student to do what he said he had always wanted to do, which was study art. He was quite brilliant. I thought I had persuaded him to do a PhD but perhaps at the end of the day an academic career didn't appeal to him either. He was a very restless man; I don't think he ever really knew what he wanted to do.'

'And what could he have done with a fine art degree?' Cobb enquired.

'Well, if he'd stuck with it and done his doctorate he could have gone into the research world, or lectured, or taken a curating job, or worked for one of the fine art auction houses like Sotheby's, but with just an ordinary degree, even the First he achieved, he would have struggled to do anything exciting.'

'If that was what he had always wanted to do, why didn't he continue with his studies?' Bould asked.

159

Dr Winterbottom was very old. His skin was leathery and deeply creased, like a deflated football, but his blue eyes were still bright and clear, the mind behind them still sharp as pins. 'That's a question I've often asked myself. From his first day he said that a doctorate was his goal but then, after he graduated, he took the summer off. The last thing he said to me was that he would be back in the autumn but that was it. I never heard from him again. It was a crying shame; he was quite, quite brilliant and I felt I had to come and pay my last respects. But now I think that perhaps it was a mistake. I'm sitting here thinking of what might have been, and what good does that serve?' He shook his head sadly, unable to understand the folly of some people.

'What year did he graduate?' Cobb asked.

'1978.' Dr Winterbottom picked up a samosa and held it up to the light as if he wasn't sure whether it was safe to eat. 'Do you know what this thing is?'

15

'I want us to toss some ideas around and see what we come up with.' The DI was addressing his team in the CID room. Outside the temperature soared and the pedestal fan was whizzing around on top speed but it was making no difference at all. Occasionally, as it oscillated in his direction for a brief moment, the air temperature dipped a milli-degree but otherwise it was about as useful as a hairbrush would be to a bald man.

Cobb loosened his tie and undid the top button on his shirt. 'Now, we know Boot worked all his life as a quantity surveyor, even becoming the senior partner in the old Mallerton firm of Swallow & Carrick, but we've discovered today that this wasn't his preferred choice of career and as a mature student he went to London to study fine art — this also appears to be where he met his wife, if what she told us was true. He was intending to undertake a PhD in the subject, and his old tutor says he was a brilliant scholar with a glittering career in front of him, but he went away for the summer and never returned. Why? Why would he turn his back on his heart's desire and take up a job that he had no real interest in? I also want you all to bear in mind that when he returned to Mallerton in the mid eighties he came back a rich man: rich enough to build himself a mini-mansion which he named after an infamous incident in the Grand National when an outsider won against all the odds. Now, the name of the house may, or may not, be significant but we've heard the man was distinctly dodgy — are we looking at some sort of betting scam here?'

'Boot was born in 1948, Foinavon won the National in 1967: that was long before he went to London. If he'd made money out of running a betting scam then wouldn't people here have known about it at the time?' Rose asked and then added as an afterthought: 'And he'd have been very young.'

'Foinavon may have just been the start of it. Suppose he just got lucky there — and luck is all it could have been — but then he got the idea there was easy money to be made. If he was able to make the right contacts he could have done all right for himself, because at that time racing was notorious for the fixing going on, particularly on the flat. Jockeys were pulling their mounts left, right and centre,' Cobb replied.

'Suppose we're looking at this from the wrong angle,' Bould said. 'We're assuming that he's named the house after the horse because he did well out of it, but could it have a symbolic significance?'

'You mean the rank outsider who came good?' Aaron said. Unable as ever to keep still, he was twirling a biro around in his fingers, tapping it on a desk every now and then and driving everyone mad as usual.

'That's something else we need to bear in mind,' the DI said. 'However, I don't want us to become fixated on a possible racing connection. It might not mean anything more than the name took his fancy. It would be good if we could find out where he was in the intervening years, the years when he made his money. However, it's so long ago I can't help but feel it's unlikely to be relevant to his death.

'Ian, have you had any joy with Swallow & Carrick yet?' Trusting that his IT expert would have something positive to say, Cobb turned to the youngest member of his team.

'Oh yes, and it doesn't make for pretty reading.' Ian Constable pedalled his chair back to his desk and scooped up a sheaf of papers covered with figures. 'It's been going down the tubes for some time and as we all know it's an offence for a company to trade when insolvent. I should imagine Peter Smith will be calling it a day before long.'

'Surely surveyors are always in demand,' Rose said. 'You don't usually hear of them going under.'

'I agree, but when you look at the figures what you find is that Peter Smith was basically running the business on his own. Boot appeared to put no work in at all but to be fair to him he didn't draw any money out either. Peter Smith, himself, was drawing barely more than a pittance, presumably because the company couldn't stand for anything more.'

'Is that so?' The DI grew thoughtful.

'If Boot never wanted to be a surveyor and only trained to please his parents, why did he go back to surveying and not continue in the arts line?' Rose wondered.

'That's a very good question, and one we need to look into. What's even more interesting is why did he buy into a firm as a partner and then have nothing to do with it? Is Swallow & Carrick some sort of front through which he laundered his money? We're going to have to look very closely at them, I think. I've already asked Neil to run a check on William Boot to see if he's got a criminal record; I think we'd better include Peter Smith in that as well. Neil, that's one for you.

'Rose, did you manage to get a guest list for the Stephen Street opening, and the electoral roll for the area?'

'I did, and I've run checks on all those invited who turned up, and that didn't take long because there were only fifteen people present. I've drawn a blank on all of them. The electoral roll for Stephen Street didn't come up with any surprises either. I'm told there were a few people who turned up uninvited but I've not been able to get names for them.'

'OK. Aaron, I know you haven't had much time to do anything about this as yet, but do you have any info on Adam Boot to tell us?'

'Not as yet. I'm working on it though.'

In an effort to invigorate his dispirited team, Cobb grew hearty. 'Let's focus on the positive. At least we're eliminating those who aren't involved. That's something. It means we can focus on a narrower field of suspects. Now let's look at the facts in our possession in chronological order, starting with what Dr Winterbottom told us. According to him Boot was a brilliant scholar who graduated with a first class degree, then he goes off for the summer of 1978 promising to return in that autumn to start his PhD but never did.

'The next piece of positive information has been supplied by Masie Hintlesham. She said

Boot came back to his town of birth in 1985 and built himself an impressive house. We need to find out where he was in between and how he made his money. We're going to dig deeper into why he turned his back on the fine art world and joined Swallow & Carrick because his actions don't seem to make any sense at the moment. And then there's something else — William Boot said his brother wasn't interested in paintings. Now that's clearly a lie of magnitude ten on the Richter Scale, and we need to find out why he told us this. It suggests to me he didn't want us knowing about Jonathan's university studies. Now why would he want to hide that?'

'What exactly does fine art mean?' Aaron asked.

'It's the study and history of painting and the different genres, amongst other things,' Bould said.

'Oh, right.' But he sounded mystified all the same.

'It doesn't exactly sound the way to a great fortune,' Bould said. 'It's the sort of degree people have who want to become museum curators.'

Behind Cobb was the white board that dominated the room. Photographs of the victims were pinned to it and in red ink all relevant information on the case filled most of the areas in between. Lines had been drawn from some blocks of text to others, highlighting connections, proven or possible, although the latter were topped and tailed with a series of question marks. The board was already jam packed with information but it was about to become more crowded as Cobb took up a red marker pen and began to write as he listed the latest information. 'Now what do we know? We know that Jonathan Boot had a degree in fine art. We know that his brother William fiddled his way to a job at Latham Hall, which had a famous art collection, so what my sergeant and I are going to do now is talk to Mr William Boot and see what he has to say for himself, but this time I don't think we'll warn him we're coming. Let's see what he's like caught off guard. I also want him to look at the guest list for Stephen Street to see if there are any names on it that mean anything to him, because it's almost certain that's where his brother was poisoned, and then after that I think we'll have a little chat with Mr Peter Smith again.

'Ian, I'd like you to take a look at the business affairs of Dukoy Holdings. Make-peace seems to think there might have been some dodgy goings on over planning permission for some big retail park Boot was involved in when he was chair of planning. He didn't tell us who the developer was, and I'm not usually a betting man, but in this case I'm prepared to stake my police pension on it being Dukoy Holdings.

'Finally — and the reason I've kept this until last will become clear as soon as you hear what I've got to say — I've had the forensic report back on the anonymous letter Adam Boot received, and it tells us nothing. There were no fingerprints. The paper is A4 computer paper sold in thousands of reams by a national chain of stationers, likewise the glue that stuck the words to the sheet. The words themselves were cut from a variety of national newspapers, and the postmark on the envelope was London W1.

'I said the report told us nothing but that wasn't strictly true. What we can learn from this is that we are dealing with a very clever killer. Someone who has covered every angle and thinks he or she can stay one jump ahead of us. I don't need to tell you all that I intend to prove them wrong.'

16

High above, in a vast sky, small clouds were building up. The heat was becoming even more oppressive.

Cobb ran a finger round his collar. 'We've going to have a storm soon,' he announced as the car crunched to a halt in the small car park. At 3.30 in the afternoon the school children had long since gone and the place was all but deserted.

Only a pre-school child being pushed on a tiny swing by her mother in the tots' playground was in evidence as the two policemen went in search of Latham Hall's project manager.

At the end of the car park was a little wooden shack housing the ticket booth; as William Boot wasn't expecting them, the officers went in to enquire over his whereabouts. The shed contained only one rather glum-looking middle-aged woman, who seemed to have no idea where their quarry was. 'I've been so busy. I haven't had a chance to move from here for the past two hours. I know it must look as if I'm not busy but that's because everyone's gone now.

You've no idea what it's like here most days. Bedlam, absolute bedlam, that's what it's like. I've asked for help, but do I get any?' This was clearly a rhetorical question because she went on without missing a beat. 'And it's so hot now. I'm sweltering in this office but in winter it's freezing. The heating here is completely inadequate. I've asked for something better but do I get it?'

She clearly hadn't finished but Cobb had heard enough, and cut across the tirade. 'He is on the premises, though, I take it?'

'Well, he was when I last saw him, but that was a couple of hours ago, as I said. I haven't even been able to go for a cup of tea. Someone should have come and relieved me, but you know what these youngsters are like.' Indignation was beginning to creep into her voice, and her cheeks flamed.

'We'll go and find him ourselves,' Cobb said, as this suited his purpose very well. He hoped to catch his man off guard.

'When you do, tell him to send someone to take over here,' she called to their departing backs.

The schools centre was empty but the number of small chairs surrounding tables littered with paper, crayons and drawings told them that there had recently been a lot of activity taking place. The room was divided almost in half by some freestanding display boards, and these too were covered in drawings of the house and gardens done by the visitors. Above the drawings, blow-ups of Victorian and Edwardian photographs showed the place in its glory days. In one, the entire household staff were arranged on the terrace and on the steps beneath them stood the outdoor workers, graded down the steps in order of their seniority.

Cobb counted twenty maids and ten gardeners, plus a butler and cook. 'The Lathams were very well-to-do once,' he observed. 'Imagine being born into this; you'd rightly think the good times were going to last forever. No wonder Henry Latham shot himself rather than face life in a council house.'

'I wonder what happened to Henry's son,' Bould said, pointing to another sepia-coloured photograph. It was a carefully posed arrangement of a middle-aged patriarch with mutton-chop whiskers standing behind a graceful, slim woman seated in a wicker chair. Her arms embraced two children standing either side of her, a boy and a girl aged about four and six. The clothes suggested the picture had been taken in the late Victorian age. 'This must be Richard Latham and his wife, so the children would be Alfred and a sister.'

Just then a spotty teenager appeared from round the back of the exhibition.

For a moment Cobb thought one of the school children had got left behind, but then he clocked the Latham Hall staff badge pinned to the green T-shirt. 'Hello, Darren,' Cobb said, reading the boy's badge. 'Do you know where we can find William Boot?'

'He's in there.' The lad nodded backwards and in the half dark they saw a door behind him.

'Does that lead into the house?' Bould asked.

'Yeah. He's got an office in there. Don't know what he does all day though. Just prats around and leaves the real work to them as what's on minimum wage,' Darren grumbled, scuffing his feet against the bare concrete floor. He had that gawky awkwardness all those of his age possessed. Then he shuffled off in just as ungainly a manner.

'I think you're wanted in the ticket booth,' Bould said to the boy's departing back.

'Yeah. OK,' the boy answered morosely and raised a hand in acknowledgement.

The officers went through the entrance and found themselves in a long corridor. Light flooded in from floor-to-ceiling windows at either end, enabling them to see the full extent of the restoration work needed. Plaster crumbled from the walls and mould spotted the ceiling. A series of doors led off the corridor at regular intervals but only one had a name plate on it. They entered without knocking.

They had interrupted something.

William Boot was standing very close to a woman who looked to be about twenty years his junior. She looked extremely unhappy, frightened almost, and as he turned away from her on hearing the door open, she ducked down and fled, brushing against Bould in her haste to get out of the room.

Boot looked furious. 'Don't you ever knock?'

'Why, was there something you wished to keep hidden from us?' the DI enquired with a lift of an eyebrow.

'No, of course not. It's just a matter of politeness.'

'Actually, I think there is something you wanted to keep hidden from us, and from your employers as well,' Cobb continued smoothly, ignoring the man's last remark.

'Don't be ridiculous. What could I have to hide?' But his voice was uncertain, and his eyes were compulsively drawn to the papers in his interrogator's hand.

Cobb took his time before replying. He walked slowly and deliberately round behind

Boot, coming up close until he was almost brushing his shoulder. Leaning forward, he spoke into the man's ear in a way that was both matey and menacing at the same time. 'You do know that it is a serious matter to lie about your past employment in order to obtain a job, don't you? I know some people might say it's just a bit of creative embroidery and there's no real harm in it — it's not like mugging old ladies, for instance — but my sergeant and me, we don't look at it like that. In fact we would go so far as to say it's obtaining money by false pretences, wouldn't we, Sergeant Bould?'

From where he had taken up position by the door, Bould replied impassively, 'Without a doubt we take it very seriously indeed.'

There was silence whilst they chose to let Boot sweat, and sweat he did. Cobb was inclined to think it was not just due to the overpowering heat.

After a time, Cobb said in a more matter-of-fact way: 'We've spoken to Lord Ragsdale.' He didn't need to elaborate.

'Oh.' Boot collapsed into a chair and sunk his head into his hands.

'So why did you do it? Why did you want this job so badly you lied?' Bould asked.

It took several goes before Boot could formulate a reply. They watched his mouth open and close like a fish on the bank, gasping for air. Eventually, he managed to speak. 'I needed a well-paid job like this desperately.' He laced his fingers together, squeezing them tight until the knuckles turned white. His head drooped over his hands in abject self-pity.

'Why?' Cobb said.

'I've got a lot of debts.'

When it became clear he didn't want to explain further, Cobb prompted him. 'How so?'

'I've, uh, I've . . . I've got a gambling problem.' He lifted his head from his hands but couldn't look the officers in the face. Instead he unlaced his fingers and spread his hands out before him, studying them as if he'd never seen them before.

'You're the gambler!' Bould couldn't help the way his words burst out.

It confused Boot. 'What do you mean, 'I'm the gambler'?' Boot repeated, and looked up in puzzlement.

Cobb spoke before Bould could say anything further. He wanted to give away the least amount of information possible at this stage of the game. 'What form does your gambling take?'

Boot returned to studying his hands and gave a rueful laugh. 'Inspector, I'd wager you which rosebud on a particular bush would open next.'

'Have you tried to deal with your problem?'

'I did go to a meeting of Gamblers Anonymous, but you know what? As I left I had a bet with one of the other members that it would rain before the next meeting.' He removed his gaze from his hands, and glanced at the officers to see if they grasped the depth of his addiction. 'I decided the only way out was cold turkey. I'd do it by myself, and I've had some moderate success, you might be pleased to learn. I still gamble now and then, but only moderately and I can control it.'

Cobb wondered who the man was trying to convince. He knew the only way an addict could kick his habit — whatever it was — was to stop entirely.

'All right, so now we know the *why* you needed this job, we come to the *how*. Was your brother involved in getting you this appointment?'

'Only indirectly. He tipped me off about it in the first place and helped me with the CV because he knew what the council would be looking for. I had some background in the field; I wasn't completely fraudulent, as I assume you must have found out. Johnny suggested it was better to stick with real people and places and came up with the idea of using Lord Ragsdale, because his place is in Yorkshire and that's far enough away to make it unlikely any council officers would have met the man or been to his property — only we couldn't have HR write to him, so we had to make out he lived somewhere else, a lot of aristocrats do, you know. They often have several houses. The fact that Johnny was a very well-respected councillor of many years standing, and known to all the officers, helped enormously because it meant they didn't perhaps look as closely at my background as they should have. Johnny was lead councillor for leisure and recreation at the time, and the appointment came under that department's auspices. Obviously that meant Johnny had a certain amount of influence and made it difficult for the head of department to say no . . . Do HR know about this?'

'Not yet,' said Cobb. 'It must be the influence of this case but I've suddenly become a sporting man. So here are your options: we'll give you twenty-four hours to tender your resignation to the council, and if you haven't done so within that time, we'll apprise Ms Golightly of the true facts regarding your past employment. Is that understood?'

Boot nodded dumbly in return, the essence of humiliation.

Feeling he'd exhausted that avenue, Cobb turned to the other matter that interested him greatly. 'Why did you lie to us by saying your brother wasn't interested in art?'

A shifty look came over Boot's face. His eyes slid away to the door as if he wished he could make a swift exit. He licked his lips. 'I didn't lie to you. To my knowledge Johnny wasn't interested in art.'

His patience had been running on empty for some time, and Cobb thought he'd contained himself very well, but now he snapped. 'You didn't know your brother went to London in the seventies to study for a degree in fine art? You didn't know he was going to undertake a PhD? Now here's something you should know, Mr Boot, I don't like people who try to obstruct my enquiries, and right now I'm minded to arrest you for just that. I could have you in a police cell so fast your feet wouldn't touch the ground.' He had the pleasure of seeing Boot, who already knew he was in deep trouble, look absolutely terrified at this threat.

'But that was decades ago! Johnny was just a young man. He didn't know what he wanted to do with his life. You know what it's like when you're a teenager.'

'Correct me if I'm wrong, but your brother wasn't exactly a teenager when he went to university,' the DI said grimly, not prepared to cut the man any slack.

'No one in our family had ever been to university before. Our father owned a shop in Mallerton, but he was ambitious for us. He thought we were bright and could make something of our lives. He was right too, you know.' For a moment, pleasure at remembering how successful in their different ways the two of them had been caused Boot to stop his narrative, and a touch of self-satisfaction coloured his words. 'Anyway, he got Johnny into a local surveying firm — Swallow & Carrick — because he knew the senior partner through the Rotary Club. Johnny went along with it because he couldn't think of anything else to do, but as soon as he could he took off for the bright lights of London. The subject of his degree didn't matter to him. He simply wanted to experience university; do the whole student thing. In his mind it was going to be non-stop parties and girls galore. The funny thing was, he found he enjoyed the studying and had a real flair for the subject; but there's no money to be made from it, and Johnny always liked money, so after he'd done his degree he came back here with the intention of getting back into Swallow & Carrick. Luckily for him, old man Swallow owed our father another favour.'

Unimpressed with this story, Cobb repeated his original question. 'Why did you say your brother had no interest in paintings, when that couldn't be the case? It's all very well saying the subject of his studies wasn't important, but there must have been some reason why he chose fine art. No one goes and studies something they have neither interest in nor knowledge of.'

Boot threw his arms open wide, in the forlorn hope of appealing to the DI's better self. 'Mr Cobb, Johnny did his degree over thirty years ago. Since then I have never heard him express any interest in art or painting. He has never been to an art exhibition or gallery or museum, as far as I know. He chose the subject because he thought it would be something easy to study. Easy to scrape through. The fact that he never went back to do the PhD his tutor tried to railroad him in to undertaking surely proves my point.'

Cobb had to admit the fact that William did indeed have a point, but he wasn't going to let the man off the hook that easily. 'Nevertheless, you lied to us when you said your brother had no interest in paintings. Now, perhaps I should explain to you the way I view people who lie. I say to myself, they've got something to hide. So, tell me, Mr Boot, what are you hiding from me?'

'Nothing! I swear to God.' The words came out as a yelp as Boot leapt to his feet, knocking his chair over in the process. He backed away into the corner of the room, as if in fear of his life. 'I didn't mention it before because I didn't think it mattered. I've just told you, he showed no interest in paintings after he returned from London, and I've no idea what he did during his university time because I wasn't there. Look, you have to believe me. You've been in Johnny's house — if he had an interest in paintings why didn't he own anything decent? He could certainly afford to buy some modest works but all he had were reproductions or cheap originals by sentimental Victorian artists. Believe me, there was nothing in his house to suggest he had even a passing interest in good art.'

'That's just the trouble, Mr Boot. I don't know if I can believe you.' It was obvious he wasn't going to get anywhere with this. Boot had decided to stick to his guns but Cobb could see from his sergeant's face that a different line of questioning had occurred to him, and he gave a nod to indicate the go ahead.

'You're in charge of applying for grants to do this place up, if I remember rightly,' the sergeant said.

'Yes, I am.'

'How much are your debts? I mean, is your salary here going to be enough to clear them?'

Boot knew exactly what was being inferred. His lips compressed into a thin line, but where they might have expected to see anger flare in his eyes, only misery and defeat showed. They watched as conflicting emotions chased each other swiftly across his face. Then the struggle was over and he addressed them with a certain defiance in his voice. 'Whatever I may have been thinking was possible, I haven't been successful in obtaining any money from external sources and so the temptation to perhaps appropriate some of those funds hasn't arisen, you'll be pleased to learn, so you've nothing you can pin on me there.'

'You seem to be admitting that you did intend helping yourself,' Cobb said. 'Perhaps we should caution you at this point if you are admitting intent to commit a crime.'

He succeeded in making William look even more terrified than ever. The man glanced wildly around the room as if planning to bolt. 'You wouldn't arrest me for a crime I haven't committed, surely. I mean, you're supposed to be looking for the person who killed my brother and his wife. Why are you bothering about something that hasn't happened and never will now? I wouldn't have said what I did if I thought . . . ' His words trailed unhappily away.

The policemen let the silence grow and the man sweat some more. Soon he'd tell them everything they wanted to know.

'Did your brother gamble at all?' Eventually Bould carried on with his earlier line of questioning.

William laughed sourly. 'Oh no, he was much too smart for that. Said it was a mug's game. Bookmakers drove Rolls-Royces, he'd say, not the punters. The only exception he ever made was the Grand National and that was because he had discovered a rather fascinating fact about betting on it. If you back every runner both ways, because of the highly unpredictable nature of the race and the odds some of the horses attract, you would very rarely lose. You may not win much, but you would usually end up a few pounds in pocket, and every now and then you stand to win quite a bit, because a rank outsider nearly always finishes in at least one of the first four places. It's that sort of race, you see: entirely unpredictable. You could never fix the National. Anyhow, that's how it was in 1967. I'd bet on the favourite and lost everything — and I mean everything. Johnny, on the other hand, backed every horse both ways to prove his point and ended up several hundred pounds in profit.'

'Is that why he called his house Foinavon?'

'In a way.' Boot's eyes shifted again. He was prevaricating and they wanted to know why.

As that answer was highly unsatisfactory and told them nothing, Cobb raised his voice. 'But he couldn't have made enough money to build his house from his winnings.'

'It was a nasty little joke at my expense. It was his way of letting me never forget what a mug's game gambling is, and how much smarter than me he was.'

'Did your brother never offer to help you out by paying off some of your debts? From what we hear, he could easily afford to,' Bould asked.

'No, and I never expected him to. He helped me get this job and said that was better than giving me money as I'd only blow it on the horses.' William gave a short laugh as he recognized the truth in that.

'But you only got the job in the last three years. Are you saying that for decades he never tried to help you? That doesn't sound very brotherly to me.' Bould sounded quite taken aback at this.

'He did try to help at first. He paid for me

to get some counselling, but eventually he lost patience.' William rallied in defence of his brother.

'Where did your brother's money come from?' The question was fired point blank by the DI.

'I don't know. That's the truth. He wouldn't say. He always said it was best I didn't know, because then I couldn't ever drop him in it. He didn't trust me, you see. I'd always got large debts and he thought I might be tempted to sell his secrets.'

The two men eyeballed each other. Boot's face was a picture of misery and Cobb had to concede that it was likely the man was telling the truth.

'All right. Now I want you to take a look at this.' He produced the guest list for Stephen Street. 'Do you recognize any of these names?'

Boot took the paper with something approaching obsequiousness and scanned it, eager to appear helpful. 'No, sorry. I don't know any of those people at all.' He handed the sheet back with obvious regret.

'Never mind.' Cobb pocketed the list. 'Just remember what I said: you've got twenty-four hours to resign before we tell the council about your non-existent work for Lord Ragsdale.'

'Not a lot of love lost there,' Bould said as they returned to the car. 'What was going on between those brothers? Councillor Boot gets William a well-paid job he wasn't qualified for and yet seems to have delighted in spending the past four decades rubbing his nose in the dirt.'

'When you've been in the game as long as I have been you'll cease to be surprised at the number of families who come over as loving and close knit, but who turn out to hate each other with a rare passion, particularly the 'we'd do anything for each other' type. They're the ones you've got to watch the hardest, because they'll be riffling through Granny's sideboard before the death certificate's been signed.'

Cobb was feeling rather touchy on the subject of families because his step-daughter had just breezed back home now the university term had ended for the summer. At Christmas, there seemed to have been some sort of rapprochement between them, and he had been filled with optimism that their relationship would at last go the way Sarah, his wife and Carly's mother, had spent nine years hoping for. The past week had put paid to that, leading him to believe that Christmas had been nothing more than a false dawn. They must have simply been overcome with the notion of goodwill to all men at the time because now, in the height of summer, she seemed to have reverted to truculent adolescence. The first thing she'd done on her return was to say hello and can you lend me fifty quid in the same breath. Just like that. When he'd asked her (not unreasonably in his book) what she wanted the money for, she'd gone into a mighty huff, stormed off and refused to speak to him for two days, after which time he discovered Sarah had lent (given her, more like) the money. Now he and Sarah were at odds with each other, and just as he had begun to win her round to the idea of a holiday.

He was too depressed to talk and the journey to their next port of call was made in silence.

17

The storm was beginning to break as they drove to Swallow & Carrick. Overhead rumbles of thunder sounded, far away and tinny, not yet full throated, as if the imminent storm was just flexing its muscles, preparing for a show stopper. A few more rumbles occurred, getting louder and closer and then without warning the clouds, dark and fat with rain, suddenly let rip. Like a balloon bursting, the rain fell in one continuous waterfall. Bould turned the wipers on to their fastest setting but even so they couldn't keep up with the streaming torrent. The road could only be glimpsed between beats of the blades, and then only for the briefest of moments.

The surveyor was in his office, dictating a report onto a handheld tape recorder as his receptionist ushered them in.

Smith seemed scared and jumpy and played for time. 'I'll just deal with this first, if you don't mind.' He pressed a button on the machine and ejected the tape. 'Amy, you can start typing this up first thing in the morning. It's not complete but I'd like it finished today. I'll do the rest later. All the names and addresses are in there.' He handed the tape and some files over and watched as she left the room before turning to the policemen. 'Now, what can I do for you?'

'We just wanted a quick word with you to check out a couple of things that are puzzling us,' Cobb said in his best matey-but-chilling voice.

He must have been on top form because Smith immediately did a fair impression of Boot by looking similarly terrified. He seemed to have interpreted the DI's smile as like that on the face of the tiger when it's looking at its dinner. He was too frightened to answer, and stood stock still, his hands hovering in mid air.

'You see, Mr Smith, we had a look at your company's financial position, and it isn't pretty. In fact it looks to me as if the shutters are going to come down quicker than autumn leaves.'

'What do you expect me to say to that?' Smith laid his hands flat on the desk as if to steady himself, and gave the officers a look of pure anguish.

'You could start by telling us how this situation has arisen. In fact, whilst you're at it you could tell us what Jonathan Boot got out of the company. He seems to have done no work and taken no money. Now I might not know much about business, but that seems a pretty strange way for the senior partner to behave.'

In the ensuing silence Cobb and Bould watched as Smith struggled with himself. A multitude of emotions flitted across his face. The DI hoped the man didn't play poker — although it might explain where the company's money had gone.

Like a blind man, Smith groped for his chair and all but fell into it. His words came haltingly. 'We've never really done very much here. Jonathan took me on because he wanted someone he could push around.' He looked up with a rueful smile. 'The temple at Delphi says 'know thyself' and I know the sort of man I am. I was a bitter disappointment to my parents, and my wife feels the same way. I don't blame them. I can't stand up to anyone. I don't like confrontation, you see. It stems from having a childhood that consisted of my parents spending their lives at each other's throats, I guess. I think it was almost a hobby with them. Anyway, by the time I was twelve, I'd had enough to last me a lifetime.' He came to an abrupt halt, and Cobb had to avert his gaze to avoid the look of misery in the other man's eyes.

'Why did Boot need someone to push around?' Bould asked quietly.

'He had no interest in surveying at all, and certainly didn't intend actually doing any. So the deal was I'd do the work and could draw all the profit as salary. He took nothing, but it stopped any speculation.'

'What speculation would that be?' said Cobb.

Smith looked up in bewilderment. 'Well, people would wonder how he could afford to live as he did if they thought he only had his councillor's allowance coming in.'

'So how did he afford to live as he did?'

'I don't know.' The surveyor shrugged his shoulders. 'He didn't tell me anything if he could help it. He offered me a partnership. I didn't have to buy into the firm, which is the usual practice. I couldn't have ever afforded to become a partner otherwise.' He paused then seemed to feel the need to make another confession. 'I've never been very successful at anything, so this was like a gift from the gods: a free partnership.'

'If Boot wasn't taking anything out of the firm, how come it's been doing so badly?' Bould tapped his notepad with the tip of his pen.

They were kicking a man who was not only down but nursing two broken legs, and it wasn't giving either of them any pleasure, but they had to be pitiless.

Any minute now it looked as if Smith would burst into tears. The words were forced from his lips. 'I'm not very good at the business side of things, and one or two surveys I did weren't quite up to scratch — '

'Meaning?' Cobb jumped into the void.

Mumbling, talking to his hands rather than the officers, Smith, who had gone so white they thought he might faint, said: 'I missed a couple of things that seriously affected the price. Word gets around once that happens, clients evaporate and insurance gets very expensive.'

'When we were here before we asked you about a row you had with Mr Boot just before he died. You told us that it was because he hadn't been to do a survey. In the light of what you've told us today, do you wish to change your earlier statement?'

'It was the truth, more or less. I wanted Jonathan to have some real input into the business. He was a well-known character, who was highly regarded locally. I thought if he got seriously involved it might restore the firm's reputation, and he could have brought in a lot of clients with all his council connections, but of course he wasn't prepared to do it. He reminded me of our agreement.'

Torture had never been in Cobb's nature,

and now he brought the conversation to a swift end. 'All right, Mr Smith. I don't think we need to ask you any further questions.' The look of gratitude he received would have been enough to make him blush if he was that way inclined. 'I'm sorry we've had to ask you these questions but we need to establish where Mr Boot's money came from, in case it's relevant to our enquiries.' He didn't usually feel the need to apologize to the people he interviewed either, but there was something profoundly helpless about Peter Smith. He recalled Sylvia Boot's words: 'Poor Peter Smith.' Yes, that just about summed the man up. He turned to Bould, who was in the process of putting his notebook away. 'Come on, Sergeant, we need to get back to the station. Good day, Mr Smith.' He would have liked to express his optimism that the financial affairs of Swallow & Carrick would work out, but he couldn't utter words he didn't have any faith in.

★ ★ ★

'What was Boot hiding?' Cobb wondered out loud, before taking a deeply satisfying bite from a chocolate doughnut.

On their return to the station they found the rest of the team were out. Price and

193

Constable were investigating a robbery where two masked men, armed with baseball bats, had broken into a property, tied the terrified owner up and systematically gone through her house, helping themselves to several thousand pounds' worth of jewellery in the process, and Rose had gone to interview the proprietor of Duckings, an upmarket dress shop which had recently been on the wrong end of several fraudulent credit card transactions.

Unable to talk to the team, Cobb and his sergeant had repaired to the police canteen and whilst Bould tucked into roast beef, Yorkshire pudding, roast potatoes and parsnips, Cobb settled for his favourite snack, knowing that in two hours' time Sarah would have his dinner on the table. He didn't want to contemplate what it would be tonight. Yesterday had been steamed haddock and the night before linguini with pesto sauce. With any luck he might get chicken this evening, which was something to look forward to until he considered what vegetables would accompany it. Broccoli and boiled spuds would be his lot, as he knew from bitter experience.

Whilst they ate, he offloaded his thoughts on the case to his sergeant. 'The money in his deposit accounts, the money that provided a fair chunk of the income that he obviously did live off, had to be obtained by illegal means otherwise why not just admit it? Why not just tell the world he's one of those lucky sods who don't need to work for his keep like the rest of us?'

'Perhaps it was because it wouldn't have gone down very well with the voters. He seems to have had an image as a man of the people, and living on unearned income rather puts you apart from everyone else,' Bould replied, setting down his knife and fork, whilst he chewed over the facts.

'Now that raises another point of interest to me: why was he a councillor? No one seems to think he did it because he had the interests of the public at heart. The only person he seems to have cared about was number one.'

'The oxygen of publicity? Some people need to be in the public eye all the time; it's what gives them a purpose for living.'

'No, I'm more inclined to think it was because that's where a lot of his money came from — backhanders and kickbacks. Power corrupts, as Churchill once said, which neatly brings me back to the idea that his money was ill gotten. We've all heard of reclusive millionaires who keep their business dealings highly secretive and are never seen in public, but Boot hardly falls into that category. His mugshot was in the papers nearly every week. He seems to have positively courted publicity in his civic role.' He became aware that Bould was distracted, his attention elsewhere, and Cobb turned round to see what had caught his sergeant's eye.

Cathy Treharris had walked into the canteen with a PCSO. She acknowledged her fiancé with a grin that was positively cheeky and a tilt of her head. Bould smiled back, and she came over.

'Just going to grab a quick coffee,' she said. 'Hello, sir.'

'How's it going, Cathy?' Cobb asked. He had a lot of time for this very bright young constable who was still with uniform but whose ambition to get into CID was well known. He wondered how that would work out when she married his sergeant because she probably would be transferred elsewhere if she did make CID. Pray it wasn't to a station far away, for he selfishly didn't want to lose Bould as well, who was far and away the best sergeant he had ever had.

'It's going just fine, sir. Things are getting a bit hectic now with the wedding just seven weeks away. You'll be getting an invite once we get round to writing them!'

'Good God, is it only seven weeks? I hadn't realized it was so soon.'

'You and me both, sir,' Bould said, deadpan, giving Cathy a sly look.

'Too late to back out now, buster,' came the stout rejoinder. 'I'll see you later. Cheerio, sir,' and she was gone.

'You've made the right choice there, Neil. I can only hope you'll be as happy as me and Sarah — just don't let her put you on any diets.'

'No chance of that; Cathy likes her food even more than I do. But to get back to Boot — even if his money was not legit, does it have anything to do with his death?'

'I don't know, but it's the fact that he has gone to such pains to hide the source of his income that interests me. Does it mean he was worried someone from his past would find him and exact revenge?'

'Someone he'd swindled, you mean? But why would they kill Mrs Boot? Do you think that means she was involved as well?'

'I'm mindful of the fact that he met her in London, where he'd gone as a penniless student and returned not only with a wife but a lot of money as well and, of course, there are the remarks he made to Artemis Dukoy. If you liken you and your wife to Bonnie and Clyde, there's only one way those remarks can be interpreted.'

'Bonnie and Cylde were bank robbers and

killers,' Bould said thoughtfully. 'I suppose it depends on whether he meant their crimes to be compared literally or not.'

'Perhaps we'd better look into Sylvia Boot's background. It's something we've not done at all yet. We may have been concentrating too much on her husband. It's a pity we can't find any trace of the letters Mrs Boot received, and it's a pity we don't know if her husband received similar letters because then we could compare them to the one Adam received just in case his letter is from some attention seeking nutter.'

They both hoped it wasn't. Almost every high-profile crime attracted the sad, lonely and deluded who had nothing whatsoever to do with the crime but wanted to claim responsibility. They were every copper's nightmare, wasting time and money.

'I'll get on to it first thing in the morning, and I'll run the check on William as well.' Bould glanced at his watch. 'If you don't mind, I'd like to get away reasonably early tonight. Cathy wants me to go round to her parents to discuss the table plan.'

A wolfish grin lit up his boss's face. 'If you've any sense you'll leave the women to that — apart from the fact they love planning all the little details of a wedding, the table plan is where many an innocent man has come to grief. It's like lambs to the slaughter. Blood will be spilt, mark my words. And it'll all be for nothing, because the plan will be changed at least six or seven times between now and then. Keep well away, that's my advice. Then you can legitimately claim it was nothing to do with you when the rows start — and they will. Listen to the voice of bitter experience. I know all about table plans.'

'Thank you, sir. I'll bear your advice in mind,' Bould replied as courteously as he could.

The edge to his voice wasn't lost on Cobb. He should keep his opinions to himself, that's what his sergeant was telling him, and quite right too. This would be a fraught enough time for him as it was. No man deserved to be plunged into a murder investigation on the eve of his wedding. He'd make amends as best he could. 'Look, go home now. There's nothing that won't keep till tomorrow and the chief superintendent will be pleased to hear we're keeping the overtime rate down.'

'Thank you, sir. In that case, I'll see you in the morning.' Bould got to his feet with alacrity and headed off, leaving Cobb to finish his doughnut alone.

18

Bould's phone began to ring as he waited for the heavy metal gates to the station yard to slide open. Glancing down at the screen, he recognized the DI's mobile number. Without waiting for the gates to open fully, he inched forward, answering his phone at the same time.

'Where are you?' Cobb's voice growled over the air.

'Just arrived at the station, sir.'

'Then turn right round and come out to Latham Hall as fast as you can.'

Bould felt that usual adrenaline rush, and his pulse quickened. 'What's happened?'

'Tell you when you get here. I'm in the Roman garden.' The line went dead.

The school holidays had begun and traffic on the roads was light so Bould reached Latham Hall within twenty minutes. The gardens didn't open to the public until ten, and he found the car park empty apart from two marked police cars, Cobb's and Dr Bolton's own cars and another two private cars he didn't recognize and ominously a black windowless mortuary van. At the far end of the car park, by the little ticket booth, a uniformed constable stood stiffly to attention, guarding the entrance to the gardens.

Bould showed his warrant card and the constable nodded him through. 'You want the Roman garden,' he said helpfully.

Even on a cloudy day the gardens were still glorious, a fact that instilled itself in Bould's subconscious as he hurried across the terrace, down the steps, through the stone arch at the far end and entered ancient Rome.

The scene before him jarred with its incongruity. For arranged in front of the perfect Roman villa were a knot of people in blue disposable SOC overalls. They were looking at something lying on the ground, and over which Dr Bolton was kneeling. A stainless steel trolley with two attendants stood nearby, waiting to receive its load. A wooden chair, tipped over on its side, lay beside one of the slender marble columns of the colonnade in front of the villa. The juxtapositioning of ancient and modern was startling. As Bould made his way across the lawn, past the circular fountain, following the clearly marked narrow path that had been designated for the use of crime scene personnel, he became aware of an addition to the scene. Something else that hadn't been there the previous time he had stood in this garden. From a horizontal cross piece of the colonnade dangled a piece of thick rope.

'There you are, Sergeant.' Cobb detached himself from the group and made his way towards Bould along the taped path.

'Sir?' Bould shot a questioning look towards the body on the ground.

'William Boot. Found hanged this morning by one of the gardening staff. Looks like he's been here all night. The boy raised the alarm and they managed to cut him down, but it was too late. Far too late.'

'Suicide?'

'Possibly. There's a note in his pocket, typed on a word processor and unsigned, so we'll have to see. I'm not sure I can imagine William as the suicidal type. Gamblers are by nature invariably optimistic.'

'I know what you mean, sir. But the letter Adam Boot got said he was next, so if this is murder then our killer's had a change of plan.'

'Assuming Adam Boot is still alive. I've got the Met checking on that as a matter of urgency. If he is, they'll offer him protection if he wants and give him protection even if he doesn't want; possibly even move him to a safe house.'

They had continued walking as they spoke

and now Bould found himself looking down at the body of William Boot. He was wearing the same clothes they had seen him in the day before, but they were damp with dew.

Bolton looked up at their approach. 'Can't do any more here. I'll have the body taken back to the lab. Looks like he died from asphyxiation by hanging, but I'll let you know more after the PM. However, I'm confident in my conclusion because you don't get more classic symptoms than this.' With one hand either side of the dead man's head, Bolton turned it to show the officers what he meant. They saw how the tongue protruded between engorged lips and how the whole face was suffused with blood.

'Will you be able to do the PM today?' Cobb said.

Bolton looked at his watch. 'Maybe, if all things stay equal. Who's going to attend from the police — will it be you?'

'If not me, then my sergeant.'

'Make it 5.30, that's the earliest I can do.' Getting to his feet seemed to cause the pathologist some difficulty. As he struggled to push himself off the ground, Cobb and Bould exchanged glances.

'Arthritis in the knees,' Bolton said curtly, seeing the looks, but his tone made it plain he thought it nobody else's business but his own.

He beckoned the two mortuary attendants to bring the trolley forward.

As the body was being lifted on to it, Cobb indicated the chair on its side. 'This fits with the suicide scenario.'

'What did the note say?' Bould asked.

'That he had nothing to live for any more, devastated as he was by the loss of his brother and sister-in-law.'

'That doesn't seem to tie in with what he told us yesterday about his relations with his family.'

'That's exactly what I thought.'

They stood under the colonnade, looking up at the remains of the rope. The knot securing it to the wide beam was expertly tied.

'Whoever tied that meant business,' Bould said. 'And all we've got is a typed, unsigned note giving a rather improbable reason for suicide. It's very iffy.'

'Isn't it just? That's why I'm treating the garden as a crime scene.'

As if on cue, a blue overalled SOCO team emerged through the archway and headed over towards the DI.

Cobb, watching them approach, continued addressing his sergeant. 'Best to be safe than sorry, and bearing in mind it's beyond doubt that his brother and sister-in-law were murdered I rather think CS Black would have my guts for garters if I didn't consider the other possibility from the word go.'

He broke off to issue instructions to the waiting SOCO team before returning to his sergeant. 'I've seen all I want to see here for the moment. I think our next port of call should be Boot's office. I'd like to take his computer away for examination — see if there is any evidence that the potential suicide note was typed on it, then I think we'll go and take a look at his house — ' Cobb flashed the dead man's house keys at his sergeant ' — and see what we find there.'

They approached the office by way of the school centre, as they had done once before. On entering the main house they saw the corridor was empty but before they reached Boot's office, his door opened and someone came out. It was the woman they had seen in there with Boot the previous day. The woman Boot had appeared to be intimidating.

She jumped on seeing the officers.

'Good morning, madam.' Cobb said pleasantly enough. 'Can I ask what you were doing in there?'

'Oh, I was just . . . just putting Mr Boot's post out.' She was flustered; her glance darted anxiously over the DI's shoulder, seeking an escape route.

'Isn't that rather pointless, all things considered?' Then seeing as how calm and unconcerned she appeared, a thought struck him. 'I take it you have heard what's happened to Mr Boot?'

'Oh yes, but I didn't know what else to do with it. Anyway, whoever takes over as manager, even on a temporary basis, will need that office and will have to answer the mail.' She was beginning to collect her wits together, and answered warmly.

Cobb reckoned she was about thirty-five, slim, and casually dressed in pink cotton trousers and a white T-shirt. Black hair, hooked back behind her ears, hung limply to her shoulders and her face was devoid of any trace of make-up.

'Are you Mr Boot's secretary?'

'I'm the general factotum. Office manager is my title, if you must know, but it doesn't mean a thing as I'm the *only* person employed here to do the office work, so I'm expected to do everything — type his letters, make him coffee, run to the post office — you name it and I'm expected to do it.' She sounded bitter and put upon.

'And your name is?'

'Jilly Warrinder.'

'Good. Well, Miss Warrinder — it is Miss, is it?' He'd noticed the lack of a wedding ring

206

but that was something else that didn't mean a thing these days.

'Actually, it's Ms. I consider my marital status to be completely irrelevant, and none of your business.'

Cobb ignored the provocative and quarrelsome tone she had adopted and indicated the door to Boot's office. 'Please step in here, Ms Warrinder. I'd like to ask you a few questions.'

'What about?'

'Shall we start with you telling us what the argument you were having with Mr Boot yesterday was all about?'

'We weren't arguing.' She was defiant, sticking her chin out and folding her arms.

'It certainly looked like an altercation to us,' Bould said as he took his notebook out.

The realization that notes were going to be made of the conversation seemed to make Jilly nervous. Her stance became less adversarial, and her gaze flickered uncertainly from one policeman to the other.

'William was just explaining to me how he wanted the paperwork filed.'

Cobb wondered if it sounded as ridiculous to her as it did to him. Sighing heavily, he walked away to the window, stretching out the time before he replied. If it made her more nervous — good. That way, they might get to the truth quicker. He let his gaze linger on the gardens without taking note of their glory for a full twenty seconds. Then he turned round so swiftly she jumped again. 'Ms Warrinder, when we arrived yesterday, Mr Boot was virtually at your throat. You looked frightened and used our arrival to run from this room. Now if you really think we're going to believe that was nothing more than a civilized discussion over office routine you need to think again, and think again fast. Of course, if you persist in being difficult I could have you taken down to the station and charged with obstructing the police in the course of their duty, couldn't I, Sergeant Bould?'

Bould looked up and said, poker faced, 'Most definitely.'

Jilly's face showed a strange mixture of defiance and fear. It was clear she didn't know if they meant it. After some hesitation she decided not to risk it. 'William was trying it on with me.' Her whole body sagged. She seemed smaller, like a deflated balloon.

'I'm afraid we're going to have to ask you to be more specific,' Cobb said.

'Oh, for goodness' sake!' she exploded. 'He wanted to sleep with me.'

'What did you say to that?' Bould asked, writing away.

'What do you think I said? I hope I don't have to tell you I refused. He'd been on at me for weeks, and yesterday he got really nasty over it. Previously he'd been wheedling, cajoling — you know the sort of thing that type of man does. He was promising me promotion. Promotion! That's a laugh. Before his brother's death he used that line a lot. 'My brother's the mayor, you know. He's a very important person in this town.' ' Her voice took on what they had to assume was meant to be an imitation of her late boss. 'It was pathetic. What sort of man tries to get a woman into his bed by using his brother in that way? Even if I'd been that sort of woman, and I can assure you most wholeheartedly I am not, did he really think I'd believe such rubbish? He might think a job with the council is the highlight of his career, but it certainly won't be mine. I've got much bigger fish to fry. This job is just a stop gap until something better comes along. God, if I thought I'd got to spend my life working for the council I'd shoot myself.'

'You're looking to be the office manageress of a more glamorous enterprise?' Bould suggested, only slightly sarcastically because sarcasm wasn't his thing at all.

She looked at him as if he was mad. 'Don't be ridiculous! I've a degree in archaeology,

209

and that's my proper profession.'

'So why are you doing this?'

'Archaeology is a very narrow and specialized field. I was doing some research work up in Durham for the university, but the grant funding was cut and that was the end of that. No job, no money. I've had to come home and now I'm back living with my parents until something better comes up, and just as soon as I can get another job in archaeology I'll be out of here — of that you can be assured.'

'All right,' said Cobb. 'Let's get back to the subject in hand. I want to be absolutely clear on this: you're saying that William Boot propositioned you. If you felt so strongly about it why didn't you lodge a complaint with personnel?' The term human resources stuck in his craw and he found himself reverting to the older, familiar expression.

'Why? Because he warned me off, that's why. That's what the showdown you interrupted yesterday was all about. I said I'd bring a charge of sexual harassment against him if he didn't back off, and he almost dared me to do it. He said I'd regret it if I did; I said he hadn't got his brother around to hide behind any more. He said it didn't matter because I hadn't got any witnesses and no one would believe me. He was so angry I thought he was going to hit me, and then you two barged in.'

'Thank you, Ms Warrinder, that's all for now.' Cobb dismissed her with civility, but she still looked far from pleased, and after an uncertain glance at Bould, flounced from the room.

'What do you make of that, Sergeant?' Cobb said absently as he read the opened mail Jilly had put on her late boss's desk.

'Whilst I know you can never tell, and she's an attractive enough woman, I would never have put Boot down as that sort.'

'That sort? You mean to try to blackmail a woman into his bed?' The correspondence contained nothing of interest and Cobb turned his attention to the desk drawer by pulling it out completely and upending the contents onto the desk. He stirred through them with his fingers, but there was nothing there he wouldn't have encountered in countless desks up and down the country.

'Not just that, sir. He didn't strike me as the sort to be interested in any woman as such. Rather cold blooded, I thought.'

'I had the same impression, but as you say, you never can tell. The more we find out about the Boot brothers the more unpalatable their behaviour becomes. Right, let's get this office sealed off and the computer taken away for examination. I want Ian to go through it with a fine-tooth comb, see what's on there. You and I are now going to give Boot's gaff the once-over.'

19

The Firs, Station Road, Mallerton was less grand than its name suggested. That was the first surprise. The second was that the small plain 1960s box of a house had been subdivided into two flats and let out. To one side of the porch were two bells, with a name plate besides each one, informing the officers that Flat 1 was occupied by Jane Smart and Robin Pellow, and Flat 2 by William Boot. What had once been the front door to the whole property now let them into a hallway that should have had at least three doors leading off it. Now only one was visible, and it was securely locked.

'This is a rum set-up. I've never seen anything like it. I'll bet they haven't got planning permission for this,' the DI said as they made their way up the staircase. At the top, instead of reaching a landing, they were confronted by a stud wall that had been extended across the whole width of the house, and another locked door. Behind it was the landing they had expected to find, with four doors leading off. The first led into a miniscule bathroom and toilet, the second into an equally tiny kitchen, and the third into the bedroom.

The two policemen stood in silence for a second, taking in the sight before them.

'Either someone's beaten us to it and turned the place over or he lived in a permanent state of something for which the word 'mess' would barely begin to do it justice,' Cobb said laconically.

'Will we be able to distinguish which it is?' Bould wondered.

The room was dark. The carpet was dark and bare in places. It was frayed along the edges and looked as if it might have been down for the past forty years. The furniture was dark. It was the type called utility, and dated from the war years; a time when necessity and scarcity meant furniture was made to serve a purpose and nothing more. The wood was scratched and dented where it had been dragged from room to room or generally mistreated over its long life. The single bed also seemed to date from the same period. It had a dark wooden frame and a thin mattress. There were papers and clothes strewn everywhere. On closer inspection the officers could see they were mostly copies of the *Racing Post*.

'Before we start, we'll check the fourth room,' Cobb said. The sight of this dismal room had left him feeling profoundly depressed.

Bould voiced Cobb's thoughts. 'It's a bit different to how his brother lived. You'd think Jonathan would have helped William out.'

'You'd think, wouldn't you? I wonder how well they got on with each other.'

'When we first met him William made out they were very close.'

'Yesterday he changed his tune,' Cobb reminded his sergeant. 'And it would appear that was more like the truth. On the other hand, perhaps we shouldn't pre-judge. Give a gambler money to sort himself out and the chances are he'll just go and blow it on another ill-starred bet. Yesterday he admitted to us he hadn't kicked the habit. Perhaps his brother was a believer in tough love.' Cobb turned away and moved purposefully towards the last door.

It opened into what must have been intended to be a lounge/dining room. It was a reasonable size and overlooked the back garden, which was very nondescript, but faced south and sunlight poured through the large picture window. Even so, it couldn't enliven the miserable state of the room. An old oak table with barley twist legs stood against one wall with two ladder-backed chairs tucked under. The seats of the chairs were padded leather but the leather was worn and scratched. The carpet was again dark, but patterned with geometrical shapes. It reminded the officers of the sort of carpets pubs use: hard wearing and able to hide stains within the pattern. It certainly looked as if it had been down for decades. Along one wall shelves had been put up and the three rows were crammed with books.

Cobb went over and took out a volume at random. 'Architecture of the Eighteenth Century,' he read out loud. 'Seems like Boot was taking his job seriously. There's more of the same.' His gaze travelled along the row; all the books seemed to be on architecture of one period or another.

Bould had wandered over to the table, on which an open newspaper lay. 'This is the *Racing Post*,' he said. 'Looks like Boot was picking his horses for today's races.' He held up the paper and even from across the room, his boss could see the choices clearly marked with an orange highlighter.

'They are today's races, are they, you're sure of that?' Cobb asked.

Bould double checked. 'Yes, they're for today. Newmarket and Sandown.'

'Interesting. So if it was suicide, it must have been a very late decision. There's not much point putting a bet on if you don't intend being around to collect any potential winnings.'

'He's marked up at least a dozen horses — if that's his idea of being in control of his gambling it isn't mine.' Bould folded the paper neatly and put it back on the table.

'It strikes me the man was a pathological liar who was completely incapable of telling the truth,' Cobb replied.

They went methodically through the room.

'Seems his only reading material was on architecture and racing form,' Bould observed, placing the last *Racing Post* on top of a heap of its brethren.

Cobb sat back on his haunches, having just taken the last book out from the shelf, leafed through it and then upended it and shook it, just in case there might be something between the leaves that would point them in the direction marked 'somewhere vaguely useful'. 'Why would anyone want to kill this man? He seems to have led an insignificant, miserable little life, dominated by his gambling habit.'

'Could it be he owed the wrong sort of people some serious money? It's one thing betting on the horses or dogs through a legitimate company, but say he'd got into a heavy poker school, or was involved in some sort of betting scam.'

'The manner of his death is all wrong for that. Cross our underworld chums and you simply disappear from sight, never to be seen again, or at least not until they start demolishing the concrete piers of motorway bridges. This was a very public execution, if that's what it was, but we must be careful not to jump the gun. It might yet be shown to be suicide. I'm hoping Bolton will be able to give us a definitive answer when he does the PM. Let's go and see what delights his bedroom holds.'

The sparse room didn't take long to check out, although Bould found something that disproved his earlier assessment of Boot's personality. Between the bed and the wall was a pile of magazines. 'Seems he did like women after all,' Cobb said as Bould silently held up a copy of one. 'At least it gives more credence to Ms Warrinder's story.'

They had left the tiny kitchen to last, and it told an eloquent tale of lonely bachelorhood.

In the cupboard were only one side plate, one bowl, one dinner plate, one cup and one saucer, and in the drawer above was one set of cutlery.

'Look at this, sir,' Bould said, standing before the open fridge door. With a nod of his head he indicated the contents. A plastic container of rancid milk, a week past its sell-by date, a small packet of mouldy cheese, a tub of cheap margarine and a packet of ham offcuts.

'Pitiful.' Cobb eyed the food. 'The difference between how the two brothers lived couldn't be greater.'

'When you look at this — ' Bould began and then stopped.

'Yes?' The DI spoke encouragingly.

'Well, I just wonder why there was no love lost between them. I know what William said about his brother helping him at first before he lost patience, but surely the mayor could have done more to help his brother than merely getting him this job? Addicts need treatment, otherwise however much money they've got it will never be enough because they'll always gamble it away, and it seems to me that the story William told about why Jonathan gave his house the name he did shows that the man was intrinsically spiteful. As far as William goes, he must have felt jealous of his brother's success, and perhaps been resentful.'

'I think you're probably right, but is this knowledge of any use to our investigation? Are you thinking that maybe William killed his brother and sister-in-law for the reasons you've suggested and then killed himself out of remorse?'

Bould leant against the cupboards, his hands flat on the work surface behind him. 'If he did, and if he committed suicide, surely he'd have put that in the note; instead he said the opposite, so it doesn't make sense.' Something had caught his attention, cutting his last word short. His gaze had fallen upon the side of a wall cupboard next to the cooker and facing away from the door. There was something taped to it, something they hadn't noticed before. A photograph. In one stride he crossed the kitchen and snatched it down. The subject matter was instantly recognizable to him. 'Look at this, sir.' He handed it over to Cobb.

'Well, well.'

The photograph showed a young man and a painting. A painting anyone from the area would recognize as being of Tewkesbury Abbey. The man standing in front of it, grinning smugly at the camera, wore a wide-collared floral shirt with a startling orange and purple kipper tie, and had brown hair tumbling to his shoulders.

'Taken in the seventies wouldn't you say, Sergeant?' Cobb turned the photograph over. On the back was an inscription in neat block capitals. Cobb read it out loud for Bould's benefit. ' 'Billy — this is what you can achieve if you set your mind to it. Johnny.' So I take it the young man in question is none other than our late mayor, and this is the missing painting.'

'What does it mean, though? He seems to be implying that the painting is worth a great deal, and yet everyone said it was just a cheap daub.'

'Everyone said, Sergeant, but suppose everyone was lying? Whatever else, this photograph must have had great resonance for William Boot, for why else would he keep it? It's got to be over thirty years old. Interesting that he kept it taped up where he did. Half hidden. As if he needed to be reminded of whatever lesson his brother was trying to teach him, but not too often.' He tapped the picture against the fingers of his other hand. 'When we get back let's see if we can get the painting identified. See who it's by and what it might be worth — and where Jonathan Boot bought it.'

'Perhaps he didn't buy it.'

Cobb looked up sharply. 'Indeed. That might be why the murderer took it. Reclaiming lost property, you could say, and what do we know of missing paintings from round here?'

Bould smiled, knowing the question was rhetorical. 'Latham Hall, and Boot was a student of fine art in the seventies. The collection was found to be copies in 1984.'

The DI nodded slowly, as if inwardly confirming something. 'Yes, it fits. There could be some connection between the elder Boot brother and Latham Hall, but I can't see what it is at present. The first stumbling block is how did he get near the collection? As the local ironmonger's son I wouldn't imagine he was a friend of the family.'

'Maybe not, sir, but he had a degree in the right subject. The thing is with fine art he could have become a curator or a valuer with one of the auction houses, something like that. That might have gained him entrance to the house to value the collection when the Inland Revenue were cutting a deal with Henry Latham.'

'Apart from the fact he only had a first degree, the Inland Revenue were involved in 1984, but Boot didn't return to Mallerton until 1985 — and even then he came back as a chartered surveyor. He wouldn't have been picked to value the collection — even if he was as brilliant as Dr Winterbottom suggested. Besides which, the paintings must have been copied long before then.'

'Well, in that case, what about Dr Winterbottom himself? Could he be the connection? He was going to supervise Jonathan's PhD studies, so he must be an expert in the field. He would have the credentials to gain access to the house — perhaps he was asked to value the collection for insurance purposes when Alfred was still alive and managed to have the paintings switched at that time. Perhaps Boot found out and took the Tewkesbury Abbey painting as some sort of payment for his silence. That might explain why Winterbottom came to the funeral; perhaps he was hoping to retrieve the missing painting. His explanation for being there was pretty weak, you have to admit.'

'Hmm, there's certainly plenty in what you say to chew on.' Cobb turned things over in his mind for a minute or so, before deciding on a course of action. 'Right. The first thing we have to do is ascertain if the painting came from the Lathams' collection before we charge down what might very well be a blind alley. Come on, let's get back to the station and I'll brief the team before I go to the hospital for the PM.'

But halfway down the drive, Cobb changed his mind. 'Let's take a look round the garden before we go. It would be too much to hope we'll find deadly nightshade growing here but let's check it out anyway.' He wasn't referring to the front garden, which was nothing more than a square of grass surrounded with a beech hedge, so Bould followed his boss round the side of the house, through a dilapidated wooden door hanging off its hinges and into the back garden.

From the small brightly coloured plastic slide, paddling pool and pink bike with stabilizers, they assumed the occupants of the downstairs flat had a young daughter which made it extremely unlikely they would find any poisonous plants growing in the garden and so it turned out to be. Indeed, there were very few plants growing at all, just a few rose bushes and a lot of rosebay willow herb already going to seed.

'We're wasting our time on this. If the killer used deadly nightshade as a source for the atropine he's not going to be mug enough to leave it growing in his garden for us to find.' Cobb was exasperated.

'I thought it grew wild in hedgerows,' Bould said.

'In that case, even if we found the plant it wouldn't help because the world and his wife could have accessed it and I'd prefer to have a smaller list of suspects than that. Come on, let's go.'

20

On his return to the station, Cobb found a voice message from CS Black asking him to drop into his office for a chat. Cobb thought he could guess what the chat would be about, and as it turned out he was right.

'Ah, Steve, come in and shut the door.' Black looked up from an enormous pile of paperwork in front of him. 'Sit yourself down.'

'Thank you, sir.' Cobb did as he was bid.

'Now, Steve, I wanted to see you about the overtime. It came down nicely at the beginning of the summer but I see it's shooting up again. You know the constraints on budgets these days.'

'Perhaps someone could tell the local crims, sir.'

Black shot his underling a steely glance. 'This big murder case you're currently working on: how's it going?'

'Not very well, sir. The body count is now up to three.'

'Three! Good God, I hope you're about to tell me you have got someone in the frame for them before the press start working the public up into a state of hysteria. The last thing I want to do is open the paper tonight to read about how no one is safe in their beds any more because there's a serial killer on the loose.'

'We'll solve it a lot quicker if I don't have to worry about overtime,' Cobb pointed out.

'Hmm. If only it were that simple.' Black picked up a sheet of paper and glanced at it. 'I see your sergeant has put in for some leave in a couple of months' time.'

'Yes, sir. He's getting married.'

'Is that so? Well, if he wants to be at his own wedding you'd better get this case closed pretty quick.'

'Without overtime? We do have other cases as well. The team is stretched all round at the moment.'

Black sighed, knowing when he was defeated. 'Keep it to a minimum,' he ordered.

'Of course, sir.' Cobb got to his feet. He knew Black's heart wasn't in this near-monthly pep talk, and how could it be when the work had to be done?

The DI had joined the force because he held a genuine desire to do something positive for society and this current penny-pinching attitude drove him to distraction. Why was he being asked if the overtime was necessary? Did anyone think he and his team routinely worked seventy hours a week or more just to pick up a bit of extra money in their pay packet? Annoyance made him bloody minded. As soon as this case was over he was going to take a holiday, come what may. It was years since he'd been away, for even when he'd got some time off, Sarah wouldn't leave her mother.

Holidays made him think of Jenny, their newly retired pathologist. She had taken herself off backpacking round the world. He smiled as he descended the steps down to his own floor. Wherever she was he hoped she was having the time of her life.

He was still smiling as he turned into the CID room and found the team waiting. The smile soon vanished as the muggy air enveloped him despite the wide open windows and the fan still beating frantically away.

'There's a message here from the Met,' Bould said as soon as he caught sight of his boss. 'They've spoken with Adam Boot and he's intending to return here tomorrow to sort out his uncle's affairs. In the meantime, he refused protection, insisting it won't be necessary.'

'Doesn't it seem odd how certain he is about this?' Rose said. 'You'd think anyone, if their father, mother and uncle had been murdered, would be a little concerned for their own welfare.'

'We need to check his whereabouts last night; see if he's got an alibi. From the time point of view, he could have killed his mother, and we could say his motive would be the money he stood to inherit. However, we can't place him in the time frame for his father's death and it wouldn't explain why he killed his uncle. William isn't likely to have left anything but a pile of debts.'

'Unless William had found out what Adam had done. He could have seen a perfect opportunity for blackmail. We know he was desperate for money. Adam could have decided to silence him,' Bould said.

'Have you run a check on William yet?' his boss asked.

'I have, and on Adam too, but I drew a blank for both. Neither are known to the police at all. They've never been so much as cautioned.'

'And I've not come up with anything either, sir, but I've still got a deal to do,' Aaron volunteered.

'All right, before we go I'd like to bring everyone up to date with what we've found out.' Cobb then briefly summarized the visit to Boot's flat and the conversation with Jilly Warrinder.

Then he turned to the white board behind

him and pinned the latest photograph up. 'Now if the painting in this photograph is the one taken from the Boots' bedroom, finding it will be the key to arresting our murderer. Your task, Ian, is to find out all you can about its provenance. Who painted it and when, and most importantly what it's worth. Get a list of the paintings that were in the Latham collection. I don't need to tell you that I'm hoping this will prove to be one of them. If it is, we're on the up.'

'How would Boot have come by a painting from Latham Hall?' Rose asked.

'Good question. William suggested that the late Alfred Latham sold the collection to fund his lifestyle and had copies made. As his son and heir wasn't aware of this — if indeed that is the truth of the matter — then the paintings weren't sold on the open market. Of course, we all know paintings are stolen to order for private collectors and never see the light of day again. However, if Jonathan bought it legitimately, then we need answers to two questions: one, why did he never admit it was a valuable original and two, when did he buy it? His hairstyle and dress suggest this photo was taken in the 1970s when Boot was still an impecunious student, yet he appears to already have it in his possession. All of which suggests that he did not acquire it legitimately.' Turning to Ian, Cobb said: 'Have you had any luck with tracing the source of his wealth?'

A shake of the head was his answer. 'No. The trail ends — or starts, depending on how you look at it — with his deposit accounts, and we're going back over two decades. Banks and building societies don't have to keep records that long, so they don't. On top of which the building society where he had his main accounts has been merged several times over the years, so you can imagine the likelihood of being able to trace anything back with them.' Ian looked disgusted with his lack of progress.

Cobb shared his frustration. 'We might never get the answer to that one, so let's not waste any more time in idle speculation for now.'

The team murmured their agreement with this then Aaron asked: 'Are we assuming that the picture was stolen by the killer? Because if so, how would he have known Boot had it if it was in the bedroom? That's not a place a casual visitor to the house would go to.'

Cobb looked thoughtful. 'No, it's not. But there is one person I can think of who might have been in Jonathan Boot's bedroom, and I think we might just go and talk to Artemis Dukoy again, and whilst we're on that particular subject — ' He turned once more to his IT and finance expert. 'Ian, have you had a chance to look at Dukoy Holdings?'

'I have, and you're going to love this. The company was only set up five years ago and appears to be squeaky clean. However, I also discovered they own a subsidiary called Pensey Development Ltd, whose directors are a Marilyn and Daphne Smith. Pensey seems to have been set up for one purpose only as they immediately got involved in a big development on the west side of Mallerton. I don't know if it's the one Makepeace was going on about because he never gave us names, but there's definitely something iffy about this. It was a big deal. I mean, we've talking millions here. Pensey purchased one hundred acres of agricultural land for five thousand pounds an acre. It was at Dellingbury, which is well and truly in the green belt and so only had a value as farm land. Total cost to Pensey: half a mil. Then they controversially got planning permission and sold it for four million practically overnight.'

'Nice work if you can get it,' Aaron muttered, and started jingling the coins in his pocket.

'Who are Marilyn and Daphne Smith?' Rose wondered. 'We've not come across them before, have we, sir?'

'No, but we have come across a Marilyn.'

Bould looked amazed at the idea his boss seemed to be formulating. 'You can't mean Bartley's secretary? She's half witted.'

'And who better to have as a company director, if the company is just a front. Dukoy could never have applied for planning permission in his own name, not with his wife a local councillor. Just imagine the public outrage if he'd got permission to build on green belt land. There would certainly have been claims of corruption. So it's safer to set up a bogus company, but they need directors who won't start demanding a slice of the action themselves. People who wouldn't be clever enough to try a spot of blackmail, or have ideas of their own, so who better than the Dukoys' solicitor's secretary? I knew there had to be some reason why a smooth operator like Bartley employed someone dimmer than a five watt light bulb.'

'We don't know it's her. There must be quite a few Marilyns around,' Ian pointed out.

'Agreed, so we'll just have to ask the right people nicely and get them to tell us. However, I would like to share a piece of information with you. When Neil and I visited Bartley's office I saw a copy of a letter he had written to Quentin Makepeace. The reference at the top was DB/MS. DB would be David Bartley and MS is his secretary. The S might not stand for Smith, but I think the odds are that it will.'

Any further discussion was prevented by Cobb noticing the time. 'I've got to go to the PM shortly so there's no time to go to Cheltenham today but I do want to speak to both the Dukoys again. I think we'll interview them simultaneously so as not to give them the chance to alert each other, or concoct a story, and so we won't give them any advance warning. I want to know more about this development, and Jonathan Boot's part in overcoming the planning objections. So here's the plan: nine o'clock tomorrow morning Neil and Rose will call at the Dukoy family home and Aaron and myself will take a trip to Cheltenham. I want them spoken to separately and leant on heavily.' He turned to leave and said over his shoulder: 'Black says keep the overtime to a minimum.' Then he stopped, turned round and said considerably more forcefully, 'I say get the job done whatever.'

★ ★ ★

He drove across town to the General Hospital where Bolton was based and made his way to the lab in the basement. There he found the pathologist just donning green paper overalls.

Bolton made a big show of looking at the clock above the door. 'Wondered when you were going to get here,' he said, although Cobb was smack on time.

'You said 5.30 p.m. and I assumed you meant it,' Cobb replied, keeping his voice even. Good grief, what was the man's problem?

'Hmm.' A look was shot at the DI. 'I'm fitting this in as a favour to you. I'm extremely busy, you know.'

'Now isn't that funny, because so am I. I've got a triple murder investigation on my hands, but I don't want you to worry about that. You just stick to cutting up the bodies and telling me how they died.' The room was cool, thank goodness. Even so, Cobb's temper was rising. Much more of this and he'd set off to Vietnam (Jenny's last-known destination) and forcibly bring her back to take up her old post.

Bolton looked as if he was about to say something, but changed his mind, his mouth opening and closing wordlessly. He picked up a scalpel, examined closely the shiny metal, and then pulled down the microphone suspended from the ceiling and addressed it instead, clearly stating the date and time and those present. He then got to work and, as far as he could, spoke only to add to the recording that would later be typed up by his secretary into the official post mortem report.

As soon as the green sheet covering the body was removed, something became obvious.

'What's that?' Cobb asked, pointing to William Boot's wrists, where some faint discoloration of the skin could just be made out.

Bolton raised the limb, turning it to see all round. 'Bruising, without a doubt.' He dropped the arm back onto the slab and leant across to check the other one. It showed the same marks.

'Is this a sign he was tied up?' Cobb wanted to know.

'Must have been with something quite soft if it was, say strips of cloth. Had he been trussed up with rope the bruising would be much more livid. We might even have seen the rope pattern on the skin.'

'Nevertheless, if his wrists were bound that makes it murder beyond a doubt.'

Bolton gave the DI an old-fashioned look. 'Providing the bonds were applied directly before he died.'

'Meaning?'

The pathologist shrugged his shoulders

and affected a nonchalant air. 'Sex games, Inspector. Some people enjoy being tied up.'

'I don't think William Boot was in any sort of relationship from evidence that's come my way.'

Bolton bridled as if offended with Cobb for denigrating his suggestion. 'Some men are happy to pay for this sort of thing, and frequently do,' he pointed out with a worldly wise air.

Cobb felt a parting of the ways with his temper. 'Look. Just tell me if you can whether, in your professional opinion, those bruises on his wrist relate to the time of his death.'

From the silence that ensued, it was made very clear to the DI that Bolton had taken offence. All his subsequent remarks were addressed to his secretary via the microphone.

After he had finished the dissection he addressed Cobb tersely. 'Death is consistent with asphyxiation by hanging. I've sent away samples for toxicology but even if there are drugs present, it won't change my opinion as to cause of death.'

'And the bruising to his wrists?'

Bolton made a great show once more of picking up each of the dead man's arms in turn and closely scrutinizing the marks.

'From the pattern and the way they extend right the way round, they are consistent with bindings of some soft material. I am satisfied that they were inflicted shortly before his death.'

'Murder, then. Thank you, Doctor.'

21

'Must have been purchased with the profit from the land deal,' Bould said as he and Rose pulled up outside the Dukoys' house.

For whereas the Boots' house was mock Georgian, this was the real thing: an elegant early nineteenth-century square in Bath stone set behind a high stone wall enclosing a beautifully kept garden full of showy blossoms in white and pale pinks that complemented the grace of the house.

'What wouldn't I give for a place like this,' Rose sighed in envy.

'On police wages this is the nearest we'll ever get, so make the most of our visit,' Bould said dryly as he parked up outside the portico.

Having checked with council staff the day before that Artemis had no meetings on, they were confident she would be at home at this hour, but even so they hadn't expected her to answer the door in her negligee.

She seemed flustered to see them.

'Were you expecting someone else?' Bould asked.

'No, no, of course not.' But the anxious

way she peered over their shoulders, scanning the drive, suggested otherwise.

'Can we come in?' Bould continued as it became apparent she didn't intend inviting them in.

'Why? I mean, what do you want?'

'We'd like to talk to you.'

She was unhappy and reluctant to comply. 'Inspector Cobb and I had a lengthy talk some days ago. I know you have been to see my husband. Really, can't you leave us alone? This is tantamount to harassment.' She was getting bolder as she went on.

Bould laughed. 'This is a murder investigation, Mrs Dukoy. As a councillor I'm sure you have a strong sense of public duty, and considering your relationship with Jonathan Boot I'd have thought you might have been keen to see his killer brought to justice.'

She'd been wrong footed, and wasn't happy. After the briefest of pauses, whilst she tried to regain some semblance of graciousness, she said: 'Yes, of course. The answer is yes to both of those points.' Then she stood aside to let them enter.

She took them into a charming drawing room, furnished very much as it would have been originally with little acknowledgement of the technology that marked the difference between then and now. There was no television, no telephone, no music centre, just a gilt-framed chaise longue, some well-stuffed easy chairs in velvet that matched the gold stripe Regency wallpaper and a couple of side tables with a scattering of upmarket magazines.

'Would you excuse me? I think I'd rather like to go and get dressed.' She made to leave the room but was halted in her tracks by Bould.

'Please stay here, Mrs Dukoy. It won't take long and we really don't mind what you're wearing.'

It wasn't as if she was immodestly dressed. The negligee was a full-length, bright red, lacy affair and looked very expensive.

Displeased but unable to argue, Artemis sat down, drawing the folds of her outfit closer to her. 'Well?'

Rose sat down unobtrusively in the corner and got out her notebook as Bould commenced his questioning.

'Ever heard of a company called Pensey Development?'

Whatever she had been expecting him to ask, this clearly wasn't it and she was flummoxed. The detectives could almost hear her mind working whilst she tried to decide which the best option was. To deny or admit? In the end, she must have decided honesty was less likely to get her into trouble. 'Yes, it's a subsidiary of my husband's holding company.'

'What about its directors, Marilyn and Daphne Smith?'

'No idea. You'll have to ask him. I have nothing to do with his companies.' Distancing herself from Gregory was only sensible for someone who wanted to keep out of trouble.

Bould had seen this behaviour many times and it told him she was rattled. 'Really? Well, let me explain the set-up to you. Dukoy Holdings create a company called Pensey Development who immediately bought some land at Dellingbury to the west of Mallerton — agricultural land in the green belt for which they paid half a million pounds. They shouldn't have been able to get planning permission for it but they did and sold it on for four million pounds. That was nice work.'

'It certainly sounds it.' She'd found a packet of cigarettes and a lighter from somewhere and lit up. 'But my husband's business dealings are nothing to do with me and I'm sure it was all perfectly legal.'

'Are you? It looks like a scam to us because it's obvious that your husband would never have been able to get planning permission in his own name because of you. Still, in your official capacity perhaps you can tell me how

241

any developer could get permission for green belt land?'

She must have decided against being mendacious, realizing how unlikely her protestations of innocence sounded, and became defiant. 'It went before the full planning committee — everyone had a vote on it so there was nothing underhand at all. If you're implying any wrongdoing then I would have thought you should direct your enquiries towards those councillors who voted the scheme through instead of harassing me in my own home.'

'You might think everything was done correctly but I would disagree. The whole affair stinks. Jonathan Boot was the chair of planning at the time, wasn't he?'

A wary look came into her eyes. 'Yes.' She got up, found an ashtray, and returned to her chair.

'And you admit to having an affair with him.'

'You know I do.'

'And you were at this planning meeting and voted?'

Now she looked up in amusement, the fear gone. 'Either you know nothing about the council protocol or you think I'm an idiot. Of course I wasn't at the meeting, far less did I vote. I thought it best to stay away just in case anyone made the connection.'

'But you were having an affair with the committee chairman.'

The wary look returned. She tapped ash sharply into the crystal ashtray. 'So? As Jonathan's dead I don't understand what you hope to achieve with this. Anyway, no member of the public knew we were having an affair.'

'No, and I'll bet they didn't know Pensey belonged to your husband either.'

She didn't reply, contenting herself with shooting him a malevolent glare instead as she took a deep drag on her cigarette.

The sound of tyres crunching on gravel caught Bould's attention. 'I think you've got a visitor.'

'I can't hear anything.' But her eyes narrowed as she took another long drag on her cigarette.

A few seconds later another familiar sound reached Bould's ears. 'I think your phone's ringing,' he pointed out helpfully because Artemis was busy ignoring the sound emanating from deep within a pocket of her negligee.

If looks could kill, he'd have been dead on the spot, but instead she was forced to pull her mobile out and answer it.

Without glancing at the screen to see who

was calling, she pressed the answer button and spoke. 'I'm busy right now. The police are here. Give me fifteen.'

So she knew who the caller was, Bould thought, and had no doubt that it was from the owner of the car that had just arrived; male, judging from her attire. She wasn't wasting any time mourning her late lover. Artemis the hunter, although this woman was hardly the eternal virgin like her namesake. This woman ate men for breakfast. 'It seems to me, Mrs Dukoy, that you and your husband and no doubt Jonathan Boot as well deliberately set out to mislead both the council and the public for your own financial ends.'

She stared him straight in the eye. 'Prove it, that's all I want to say. Prove it if you can.'

'So you don't deny it then?' This was a surprise; he had expected vehement denials.

She shrugged her shoulders. 'My hands are clean. The deal was with my husband's company. I am not a shareholder and I did not attend the planning meeting, so if you want to prosecute someone it should be him and not me. Jonathan Boot is dead and so he can't say anything incriminating and you can't take any action against a dead man. The deal's done — why don't you let it go?' She began to warm to her theme. 'Come to that, I don't understand why you're bringing this up now, years after the event. Don't the police have better things to do than waste their time on this? It's yesterday's news.'

Bould's countenance became grim. 'I don't much care for your attitude, Mrs Dukoy. We're investigating something rather more serious than a dodgy planning deal. People have been murdered and we are trying to find out if the Dellingbury land has any bearing on those deaths. If you know anything of relevance to our enquiries I urge you to share your information with us.'

'Well, I don't, so I can't.'

The two eyed each other, but she was defiant. Bould changed the subject: 'What do you know about a painting of Tewkesbury Abbey that Councillor Boot had on his bedroom wall?'

Artemis looked blank, as if the effort of following this conversation was beyond her. 'Nothing. I never went into his bedroom.' The penny dropped. She sat bolt upright. 'For God's sake! His wife was always at home. You don't seriously think we — You do, don't you?'

'I don't think anything. I just want to know if you ever saw this painting.' He handed her a copy of the photograph.

She studied it with curiosity. 'Who's the

man?' Her question sounded genuine.

'It's the painting I want you to look at,' Bould said, ignoring her enquiry, but not surprised she didn't recognize her late lover. Recent newspaper photographs had shown Boot to be a man gone to seed with badly dyed black hair worn over-long for his age. He looked as if he had lived the high life a little too well. There was no resemblance to the young man with the painting.

'No. I've never seen it at the Boots' house, but then I rarely went there. Occasionally Jonathan would have a party and invite some or all of the councillors and then I'd go, but otherwise we met elsewhere.' She handed the picture back.

'What about William Boot?'

'What about him?'

'Did you know him well?'

'I don't know him at all. I know Jonathan has a brother but I've never met him.'

'Not even at one of the Boots' parties?'

'No. I don't think they were very close. Jonathan, if he did talk about William, which wasn't very often, was scathing about his brother. He said William was a fool, a mug, who would never make any money, and consequently they had very little to do with each other. They moved in very different circles. Jonathan, being a very successful man, only liked to surround himself with people who were equally successful.'

'Money was very important to the mayor from the sounds of things.' It was an observation. One of the open-ended statements the police were taught to make in order to get witnesses or suspects to tell them more than they intended.

He'd touched a nerve. Artemis smiled secretly, as if she knew a joke but wasn't about to let the officers in on it. 'Oh yes, you could most definitely say that of my dear Jonathan. He liked the best of everything — but then, don't we all?' Her voice was ironic.

Bould decided it was time to unsettle her composure again. 'William Boot was murdered yesterday. Can you think of anyone who would want to kill him?'

Artemis gaped, open mouthed. The colour drained from her face and her eyes widened in dismay. 'Are you sure?' she said, and then seemed to realize it was a ridiculous question to ask the police. 'No, I mean, why would anyone kill William? He was a nobody — I mean, he was completely insignificant. It must be the work of a maniac. Who in their right mind would go around killing an entire family? Why would anyone do such a thing?'

'That's what we would like to find out. Are

you aware of anyone with a grudge against the Boots? Did Jonathan ever say anything, anything at all, even if it was almost a throwaway remark, about having an enemy?'

'No. No.' Her denials were vigorous, voice rising shrilly. She lit up another cigarette with shaking hands. 'All these deaths can't have anything to do with the Dellingbury land — can it? Please tell me you don't think it's to do with that.'

Was she worried because she might be next on the list? Bould ignored her question. He smacked the picture he'd just shown her against the back of his hand. 'Did he ever mention paintings to you, or discuss art at all?'

If he'd asked if they had discussed existentialism she couldn't have appeared more stupefied. 'No, why would he? I know nothing about art, and care even less. He knew that, and I don't think he had any interest in art either. OK, he had a few paintings on his walls but people do that because interior designers tell them to, not because they care about paintings. Besides, it wasn't his mind I was interested in. Nor, I may add, was it my mind that interested Jonathan.'

Bould was satisfied she was telling the truth. He could well believe she got all of her cultural knowledge from the pages of the Sunday supplements. 'Very well, Mrs Dukoy. I don't have any more questions for now, but we will almost certainly want to talk to you again.' He got to his feet and Artemis followed his example with considerably more enthusiasm than she had previously shown towards anything else since the police had arrived. As she hurried them from the room he handed her the usual list of phone numbers for the CID team. 'If you do feel you want to tell us anything, please contact me or any one of my colleagues any time, night or day.'

'Of course.' She painted a bright smile on her face, as if remembering she was supposed to have a sense of civic duty, and slammed the door behind them.

'Just a minute, Rose.' Bould held up his hand to stop her heading straight for the car. 'I didn't hear her visitor drive away, so let's see if we can find him.'

They followed the curve of the drive round the back of the property and found it opened out into a courtyard which had once housed horses and carriages and now housed cars.

A flame-red Ferrari was parked in the far corner and a man lounged against the wing.

Bould stopped short. 'Good morning, Mr Bartley, we seem to have a habit of running into each other rather a lot.'

The solicitor looked up, unfazed. Indeed, he seemed amused. 'Artemis said the cops were here, and as being forewarned is such a useful thing I don't share your incredulity, Sergeant Bould. It is Sergeant Bould, isn't it? I pride myself on my ability to always remember names even if I've only met the person once before years ago. It's a gift I have.' He smirked in a very self-satisfied way. 'Now if you're leaving, I'll make my entrance. Mustn't keep a lady waiting — don't you know it is bad manners? Very bad manners indeed.'

22

At almost precisely the same time that Artemis opened her door to Bould and DC Cadoxton, Cobb and DC Price were entering the Cheltenham offices of Dukoy Holdings.

Alison Spencer, Gregory's PA, took them into her office from where she phoned her boss to inform him of their presence, and although they couldn't hear what he said, Alison's responses and carefully neutral tone and expression suggested that Gregory was far from pleased.

After she returned the phone to its cradle she switched on her most professional smile and invited them to follow her up to Mr Dukoy's office.

'Good morning, sir.' Cobb strode into the room.

'Morning,' was the short reply he received. Dukoy was standing by the window drinking a cup of coffee.

Cobb thought he looked older and sicker than the previous time they had met, and that had only been a few days ago.

Having drained his cup, Dukoy raised an eyebrow in enquiry at Cobb, who decided to let the silence develop just to unsettle the man. When he judged it long enough, he said: 'We want to talk to you about a business deal a company of yours did some years ago.' Out of the corner of his eye he saw Aaron had discreetly stationed himself in a corner of the room and was beginning to take notes.

'Oh yes?' The tone was cautious and something closed down in his face.

'Yes, and I don't think you'll have a lot of trouble recalling the details because it's the biggest deal this company's ever done.'

Both men waited for the other to say something, and when it became apparent Dukoy wasn't going to lead, Cobb continued: 'Dellingbury. A company called Pensey Development of which you are the only shareholder, purchased some agricultural land there at a very advantageous price and somehow managed to get planning permission before selling the lot for a substantial profit. Is this ringing bells?'

Dukoy decided to play for time, to bluster. 'Pensey is a separate company with its own board of directors. They have a free hand to do what they consider best. I have no more than a passing interest in it.'

The expression on Cobb's face clearly said 'pull the other one'.

Dukoy decided to make a concession. 'As it

happens, I do remember the deal in question. Pensey paid the going rate for the land, Mr Cobb, and I think you need to remember that. The deal was entirely above board.'

'The purchase may have been, but no one I've met can explain how they managed to get planning permission for green belt land.'

'Anyone can apply for planning permission. It's up to the relevant council to decide whether to grant it or not. In this case it went before Mallerton District Council's planning committee and the elected members voted in favour as is their prerogative. Of course I was pleased — I'm hardly going to deny it — but it was all done openly.'

'Do you know something, I doubt very much whether there was anything open in this affair. You knew full well you wouldn't be granted planning permission because of your wife if nothing else — and that's not to mention the fact that it was green belt land — so you set up this other company in order to bamboozle decent members of the community.'

'Have you been talking to that bloody troublemaker Quentin Makepeace? I've tried to be patient with him, but any more of this and I'll see him in court for slander and defamation. I mean it.' The developer's tone was indignant, and a tint of colour touched his cheeks.

'I'm sure you do. After all, you and Jonathan Boot had the same solicitor in David Bartley, and I've seen the letter he sent Mr Makepeace on Councillor Boot's behalf.'

'He also sent him the same one on my behalf.'

'Quite frankly, sir, I'm impressed with your nerve, particularly as you previously stated you didn't know the man. I think you are in very serious trouble indeed. I'm thinking of any number of charges that might be brought, and your wife is also heading for the courts.' He was pleased to see the look of fright on Dukoy's face. Good. He'd squeeze the scoundrel till his juices ran clear. 'So tell me about the directors of Pensey, Marilyn and Daphne Smith. Who are they?'

There was no point fighting on. A sensible man always knows when to throw in the towel. 'Marilyn is David Bartley's secretary and his occasional bit on the side to use an old-fashioned term, and Daphne is her sister.'

'I've met Marilyn.' It was amazing how much intent could be conveyed in such a few words. 'How does her sister's brainpower compare?'

Dukoy allowed himself the briefest of smiles. 'Believe it or not, Mr Cobb, Marilyn is the more intelligent one of the pair.'

'Good grief. In that case I'm not even going to ask you if they took any part in running the company.'

'No, they were just names to satisfy Companies House and the legal niceties.' He hesitated and looked all round the room before finally lifting his eyes to meet Cobb's. 'What are you going to do about this?'

'I haven't decided yet, but tell me something else. I presume Makepeace had no idea about Pensey's connection to you.'

'That's right. He was simply annoyed about the development taking place on green belt land.'

'Was he the only person who made a fuss?'

'Funnily enough, he wasn't. We did have trouble from a rather unexpected quarter. The farmer who sold the land, and who was perfectly satisfied with the deal at the time, contacted Pensey after he read about the development in the local paper. In the article it was stated the land had been sold on for four million pounds and the bloody man thought he should have a cut of the money. He engaged a solicitor who wrote to Marilyn saying if he hadn't sold Pensey the land in the first place we wouldn't have made any money from the deal, which is undisputable, but without planning permission it was only worth what was paid at the time. He couldn't complain, so Bartley wrote back telling him to get stuffed.' Fear of court proceedings had instilled a deep desire in Dukoy to co-operate. Cobb had more than once observed how often it was the case.

'That's very interesting.' Cobb rubbed the side of his nose, as he always did when he was thinking. 'I'd like the name and address of this farmer.'

'I can give you that off the top of my head.' Dukoy couldn't hide his relief now that the DI's attention was focused elsewhere. 'It's Simon Purslow, Bank End Farm, Dellingbury.'

'I take it from what you've just said that you didn't give him any extra money and Bartley's response was the end of the matter?'

Dukoy shot Cobb a disbelieving look. 'Of course I didn't. All's fair in love and war as they say. He was perfectly happy with what he got at the time. It's astounding how greedy some people can be.'

'Yes, we see rather a lot of that and its consequences in the police.' Cobb was at his most deadpan. Obviously Dukoy didn't consider his own dealings to have been dictated by avarice. It was time to get heavy. 'Anyway, sir, I'd like to get back to the little question of how you managed to get planning permission. Please don't try to fob me off with any more nonsense about how it was all honestly done because it went to committee. The rules for development in green belt areas are strict and I'm amazed to discover you got it, particularly on that side of town. If it had been to the south or east of Mallerton that might, and I can only stress, *might* have not seemed so outrageous but at Dellingbury!'

Dukoy valiantly did his best to defend his actions by taking refuge in pomposity. 'If I may say, Mr Cobb, Mallerton was crying out for this development. It's created hundreds of new jobs and provided a much-needed shot in the arm for the place, and I can only reiterate there was a full vote in public. It's not for me to comment on the actions of the councillors; you'll have to ask them why they gave permission.'

He couldn't really believe what he was saying, surely? On the other hand, Cobb had interviewed more than his fair share of villains who seemed to genuinely believe their actions, however heinous, were beyond reproach. It was with difficulty that the DI kept his temper. Dukoy's argument was outrageous. 'What was Boot's price for fixing the vote?'

'I would say ask him yourself, but as he's dead, you can't, so if I say there was no price that should be the end of the matter, surely.'

It was like swordplay without the swords, and Cobb responded likewise. 'We have got access to all his financial transactions.'

Dukoy relaxed visibly and laughed. 'And you haven't been able to find anything that leads back to me or you wouldn't be pussyfooting around.'

'Maybe not, but you have just confirmed what we suspected. Not that I'm in the slightest bit interested in your dodgy deals unless it's directly relevant to my murder investigation so for the moment I don't intend pursuing this matter any further, as long as you co-operate fully with me in every respect.'

Dukoy was looking happier now, and pressed the button on the internal phone. 'Alison, bring up some fresh coffee for me, please.' He turned to Cobb. 'I would venture to suggest that if Simon Purslow was going to kill anyone it would be me, and possibly the mayor, but I can't see why he would kill his wife.'

Cobb sighed. 'Yes, I think that is fair comment. Did you know William Boot well?'

'I've never met him. Why?'

'He's dead, sir. We have reason to believe he was also murdered.'

If Dukoy's reaction was play acting, then

Cobb would have been the first to admit he was a great loss to the Royal Shakespeare Company. 'Dear God, this is getting beyond a joke.' Dukoy sank into his chair and stared out of the window. 'The mayor I might understand. There's no point in denying it, the man was as bent as a butcher's hook. But William and Jonathan had virtually nothing to do with each other. I know Jonathan helped William get a job with the council, but that's hardly a sin. That sort of thing must happen all the time, and if the man was qualified for the job I can't see the harm in it, but as far as I'm aware, they led completely separate lives. I thought it dreadful when I heard about Sylvia, but William as well. What's going on? Does someone have it in for the whole Boot family? If I was Adam Boot I'd be very worried indeed.'

'So you know the son, do you, sir?'

'I know of him. We've never met but Jonathan has mentioned him from time to time. He was very proud of the boy. Bright and making a lot of money for himself.'

'Yes, I can imagine that would please his father.'

'It must be the work of someone who is mentally unstable — wiping out one member of the family after another, and in such horrible ways . . . How did William die?'

'I'm not at liberty to say at the present time, sir.'

'No? Oh well, I have to say, speaking purely selfishly, this makes me feel a lot happier.' Dukoy was beginning to recover his nerve and looked up to see if Cobb understood what he meant, but the DI was impassive and so the developer felt bound to explain himself. 'Obviously, whoever is responsible has something against the Boots and no one else.'

'Interesting, though,' said Cobb, 'that you've just implied that up until now you thought you might be next on the list, because that brings us back to Dellingbury.'

'Well, yes, no, I don't know. I didn't mean — '

There was a knock on the door and Dukoy seized upon the interruption as a drowning man might grab at a passing lifebelt. 'Come in.'

It was Alison with the coffee. As she handed a fresh cup over to her boss, she glanced apologetically at the detectives as if she felt she had breached the usual rules of hospitality by not offering them any.

The DI waited until she had left the room before continuing his interrogation. 'Well?' he demanded. 'Why do you think William Boot's death leaves you any safer?'

Dukoy looked like a rabbit trapped in the headlights of an oncoming juggernaut. His mood had been up and down alarmingly. Now he opened his mouth a couple of times in an attempt to formulate some little speech, but failed. Beads of sweat spangled his brow and the cup rattled against its saucer. 'All right, I'll come clean. Boot took a large backhander — '

'How large?'

'Three hundred thousand pounds.'

Out of the corner of his eye Cobb saw Price's hand stop in mid flow from note taking. Even he was surprised at the amount.

'Why didn't this show in his bank statements?'

Dukoy looked at Cobb as if he was stupid. 'I didn't give it to him in cash! No, he wanted a little holiday home somewhere where he thought he could hobnob with the rich and famous, so the arrangement was I bought him a villa near Marbella. There was some cash involved, of course, because he had to grease a few palms along the way.'

'To get it through committee?'

'Yes, but I don't know the details.'

'We've gone through all of Boot's personal details with a fine-tooth comb, yet we've not discovered anything about this villa in Spain.'

'No, you wouldn't. It was all very

hush-hush as you might imagine. The deeds, and all the other legal documents, are with my bank. Although the villa is now in Jonathan's name, the original purchase was in mine. We were very careful to — ' He foundered, desperately trying to find a word that wasn't pejorative to describe the situation.

So Cobb helped him out. 'To keep your corrupt deal hidden.'

For his help he received an angry look from Dukoy. 'Call it what you will. But to tell you the truth, I did wonder, when I heard about Jonathan's death, whether Simon Purslow was behind it. He was very angry indeed about the deal. But William's murder couldn't be anything to do with Purslow.'

'Do you have any thoughts as to who might be responsible for killing three members of the Boot family?'

'No no. You've got to believe me. My only involvement with Jonathan Boot was to do with the Dellingbury land. I never met William and I only met Sylvia a couple of times.' He drained his coffee, dropped the cup onto his desk and began to prowl around the room nervously.

'David Bartley acted as solicitor to both you and Jonathan — where does he fit into all this? Did he take a backhander too?'

Dukoy stopped and turned to face the DI. He gave a short laugh. 'Solicitors don't need to take backhanders. They just charge very exorbitant fees. David Bartley does, at any rate. He doesn't need to do anything that might be considered shady to fund his living the *dolce vita*.'

'But the fact he willingly lets his secretary be used to front bogus companies . . . ' The rest of the sentence hung in the air. Cobb didn't need to spell his thoughts out.

'It means Bartley feels able to charge us double what he'd charge his other clients — and he doesn't undercharge them.'

23

As Cobb passed through the station's waiting area on his return, anxious to brief the troops, he was hailed by the desk sergeant. 'A Joan Cashmore is here to see you, sir,' he said, jerking his head towards a woman sitting in the middle row of five rows of plastic chairs. She sat alone. The rows in front and behind were full of an assortment of the local population, some of whom looked like respectable members of society and some who most definitely did not, but Joan Cashmore sat with a quiet, if forlorn, dignity all by herself.

She was a woman of indeterminate age, with grey frizzy hair scooped back from her face with an Alice band. Her skin was taut and shiny, with the red blotches of rosacea on her cheeks. An oversized handbag sat on her lap, and she clutched it tightly, as if fearing it would be stolen from under her nose if she slackened her grip.

Cobb walked over to her, leaving Aaron to banter with the desk sergeant. 'Miss Cashmore?'

'Yes, that's me.' She blinked at him and smiled shyly.

'Won't you please follow me? I'll find us somewhere private to talk.' He had been able to place her name immediately. She was on the committee of the Stephen Street Community Centre: the last-known place where Boot had eaten before he died. Cobb was very keen to hear what she had to say.

He took her into one of the informal interview rooms, the ones they used to put witnesses at ease, not the ones they used to interrogate suspects. It was still a windowless cell with just a desk and a couple of chairs, but it had a grey carpet that matched the walls and the chairs were chrome and padded fabric (grey, naturally) and were actually quite comfortable to sit on.

'Please sit down, Miss Cashmore.'

Cobb went round the other side of the desk and seated himself. 'What can I do for you?'

'It's about the day the mayor opened our community centre. One of your officers — I can't remember her name — interviewed me about it. I thought I told her everything I knew at the time, but yesterday I was having tea with my friend Pauline Short and she made the tea rather too strong for my liking. Well, I said something to her about this, and that made me remember something the mayor said at the buffet we had after the ceremony. He was awfully good, you know.

He made a wonderful speech and thanked all the committee for their hard work. Sometimes people forget to thank everyone, but Councillor Boot was a real man of the people. We adored him. You've no idea what a shock his death was to us all.'

Cobb drew a deep breath and resisted the urge to shake her. 'Miss Cashmore, could you just let me know what it was the mayor said?'

She immediately began to lose confidence in her decision, and became flustered. 'I don't know if it's important but I thought I'd tell you because I know he was poisoned and this might have something to do with it, but I do hope I'm not wasting your time.'

The DI smiled sweetly — at least he hoped it looked sweet from where Joan was sitting. 'I can assure you, Miss Cashmore, that whatever you say is unlikely to be a waste of time.' He decided to prompt her. 'You say it was during the buffet?'

She nodded vigorously. 'Yes. He'd just taken a sip of his tea, and I saw him grimace as if it didn't taste very nice. Of course, he was far too much the gentleman to actually complain, but I could see something was wrong. So I asked him if his tea was to his satisfaction and he said it was just a bit too strong for his liking. He was very gallant about it, and said he liked his tea quite weak because otherwise he found it rather bitter.'

'He said that? The tea was bitter?'

'Well, he implied it rather than actually said it, and I'm glad because Laura Bistley had gone to such trouble with the buffet. She was up half the night, you see, cutting sandwiches and baking scones, and she would be mortified — absolutely mortified — to think she had let the side down by brewing tea that upset the mayor. The odd thing was I thought the tea was rather on the weak side. I don't like it strong, you see, and I would have been the first to notice if it had been stewed.'

Cobb beamed in genuine gratitude at the woman. 'Thank you very much, Miss Cashmore. You have helped us more than you could possibly imagine.'

'I did the right thing in coming?' she breathed in relief, and sounded positively giddy.

'You did indeed. In fact, I'm going to get the nice DC Cadoxton, whom you saw before, to take your statement but before that I'd like to ask you one or two more questions.'

'I'll do anything I can to help.' She sat upright, like an obedient dog.

'How many people were present?'

She frowned in concentration. 'It's hard to say. Twenty or maybe twenty-five, it would be around that number. We invited a lot more — all the councillors — but they are such busy, busy people only the mayor could spare the time to come and that was only because we booked him months in advance. I know we are only a little community, but community spirit is very important these days, don't you agree?'

'I do indeed,' Cobb agreed gravely. 'And had all those who were present been invited?'

'I suppose so.' She sounded doubtful. 'I didn't know all of the people; I knew the head of community activities from the council because she gave us a lot of help and support in setting up the centre. And I know the committee members, of course. We didn't check invitations at the door, so anyone could have come in. It's a community centre, you see. The doors are always open for anyone to walk in.'

'I see.' What a pity they hadn't asked to see the invitations. It might have made his job just that little bit easier. 'I'll just go and get DC Cadoxton. Please wait here.'

Running up the stairs to the CID room, Cobb felt a peculiar mixture of optimism and pessimism. On the one hand, they were getting somewhere with the case. It looked as if the atropine was in the mayor's tea. That meant the killer had been there. On the other hand, the list of guests had yielded nothing. That meant the killer had walked in off the street. It could have been anyone.

Having sent Rose down to take Miss Cashmore's statement, Cobb went to his own office with a view to reading through the case file until she had finished her task. Much as he wanted to have a brainstorming session with his team, there was no point if one of them was absent. No sooner had he settled down than his phone rang.

It was the desk sergeant again. 'Now I've got a Mr Adam Boot here to see you, sir.'

They were coming thick and fast this afternoon. 'Right. I'll be down. Find me an interview room and put him in there.' He put the phone down and then immediately snatched the receiver up again, punching in an extension number as he did. 'Bould? Good. Adam Boot is downstairs. Let's go and talk to him, and on the way you can tell me what you found out this morning.'

At the top of the stairs he met his sergeant, and by the time they reached the ground floor Bould had acquainted his boss with the gist of his meeting with Artemis.

'So David Bartley has replaced Jonathan Boot in the good lady councillor's bed, has he? Talk about partners in crime! There's something almost incestuous about the relationship of the Boots, the Dukoys and Bartley.'

They went through into the reception area, and approached the desk.

'I've put him in room three, sir,' the desk sergeant said, breaking off from a heated argument with a burly, heavily tattooed, shaven-headed man.

'Thanks.'

Leaving the sergeant to resume his row, Cobb punched the security code into the door's key pad and they passed back into the main body of the station once more and made their way to interview room three. It was identical to the one he had seen Joan Cashmore in: small, cramped, with light grey walls, ceiling and carpet. It was meant to be soothing, but seemed simply anonymous.

It also seemed smaller than the other because a tall, slim man was pacing up and down, almost filling the entire space. He stopped as the door opened and Cobb and Bould walked in.

'Good afternoon, Mr Boot. Won't you sit down?' Cobb said.

Adam looked around as if searching for a chair, and then shook his head. 'No, it's all right. I won't be long. I just wanted to let you know that I had arrived. I know you won't be releasing my uncle's body just yet but I thought I'd better sort out his things. Do whatever needed doing.'

'Did he have any friends you need to contact?' Cobb asked.

'No.' Adam looked away. He looked up and down and into the corners of the room. He was thinking.

Cobb waited.

Mind made up, Adam looked straight into Cobb's eyes. 'I don't know how much you know about my uncle but I'm guessing you've been to his place and seen how he lived. He was a chronic gambler. Years ago, my father tried to get him sorted out. Gamblers Anonymous, psychotherapy, all that was available, and he was happy to pay for it. But gambling is an addiction, like drugs. You have to want to give it up and my uncle didn't want to. I don't think Father ever understood that and in the end he got exasperated with William and all but washed his hands of him. It was tragic, really. William had brains; if he could have got to grips with his problems he might have been a very different person with a very different career and lifestyle.'

Cobb preferred not to get involved in idle speculation about how William Boot's life could have turned out. If only . . . 'Where are you staying?'

'At Foinavon. It's still my family home, for the time being.'

'We'll post a uniformed constable at the property.' Cobb held up his hand as Adam opened his mouth to protest. 'Three members of your family are dead. You, yourself, received an anonymous letter stating you would be the next victim. I don't care what your thoughts on the matter might be — whilst you're here your life could be in danger and you will have police protection, like it or not.'

'But that's the point, Inspector. The letter said I was next, but it was my uncle who was next.'

'Yes, I am aware of that. At the moment I have one or two ideas about why you were sent that letter. It could well be what magicians call misdirection. Get us looking in the wrong place and whilst we are doing that the killer has a clear run.' He fished the copy of the photograph out of his pocket and passed it to Adam. 'Is that the painting of Tewkesbury Abbey you remember seeing in your parents' bedroom?'

Adam grinned as he gave it the once-over. 'Just look at my father! No wonder they say the seventies are the decade fashion forgot. What did he look like?'

'You recognize him?' Bould had appraised Cobb of the fact that Artemis hadn't.

'Yes, I've seen a few old family photographs from that time. Not many, but enough. It was before I was born, and that's probably why the age fascinates me so. Didn't you find that with your parents? I think all children say thank God we never dressed like that, but I suspect my own children, if I ever have any, will one day look at photographs of me in the same way.'

Adam couldn't know that was another 'if only' for Cobb. If only his precious daughter hadn't died within hours of birth. Still, look on the bright side; at least he'd be spared the humiliation of her laughing at photographs of him in his youth.

He'd have given his right eye for that humiliation. And his left as well.

'If we could just get back to the matter in hand. The picture — is it the one from your parents' bedroom?'

'Yes. It was definitely there all through my childhood.'

'Thank you, sir. That's a great help to us. Do you have any idea where it came from?'

'Where it came from?' Adam repeated the question with a puzzled frown.

'Yes — where they got it from.'

'No. As I said, it was always there, as far as I can recall. So I wouldn't know where it came from.'

'Your parents never said anything, anything at all about it? Please think hard, Mr Boot. It is very important.'

Something in Cobb's tone got through to Adam. He stared long and hard at the DI. 'This has something to do with their deaths, doesn't it?'

'We don't know,' Cobb answered truthfully, 'but we think it may well be of relevance.'

'Then I'm sorry I can't help you. I really wish I could.' The picture was handed back somewhat reluctantly, as if Adam felt the answer to the mystery lay within it. 'Have you found it yet?'

'No, but I think if we find the painting, we find the person who killed so many members of your family.'

24

Having made arrangements for Adam's security, Cobb started to make his way to the CID room, until rumbling from his stomach reminded him he hadn't eaten yet. A glance at his watch told him any hot food still left in the canteen would be inedible by now and that the sensible thing to do would be to grab a sandwich.

The canteen was still heaving when he got up there and the only sandwiches left were ham and tomato or tinned salmon. He chose the ham, chiefly because the presence of tomato made him feel virtuous. Even a couple of slices had to count towards his five a day. At least there were plenty of doughnuts left. He loaded a dinner plate with half a dozen, feeling in the mood to treat all his team as they were making some progress now.

By the time he got back down to the CID room, everyone was assembled, including Rose.

Setting the plate of cakes down, Cobb invited them to get stuck in whilst he and Bould filled them in on their morning's work.

As soon as Bould had finished, Ian stepped

forward. 'You asked me to get an inventory of the paintings in the Latham collection. This came through just before you got back. He held up the print-out of an email. 'It's from the Exmel Insurance Company — they were the last company to insure the collection — and in 1960 a full valuation and inventory was undertaken. One of the paintings was by Sir Lawrence Alma-Tadema, and guess what it was called?'

'Tewkesbury Abbey,' said his boss with great satisfaction.

'That's right, sir.'

'A painting by Alma-Tadema would be worth a hell of a lot,' said Bould. 'No wonder Boot looks so pleased with himself in that photograph. But it's not his usual subject matter. I didn't realize he'd painted the abbey.'

'Never mind that,' the DI said. 'I don't care if this Alma whatsit chose to paint Scotland Yard in the buff. Just as long as we are sure it's the same painting, that'll do me.'

'Then you're going to be really pleased to know they photographed the paintings for identification purposes at the same time, so we should be able to match it up without any problems,' Ian informed the team.

'Excellent, and the son says he remembers it being in their house all his life. We'll get the painting formally identified and a statement from Adam. The thing is: how did Boot get hold of it? So our next problem is to work out what connection Boot had with Latham Hall. Whoever copied and switched the art would have needed a considerable amount of time alone with the collection. That would have to be someone with an unimpeachable reputation as an art historian. Neil has suggested that perhaps Dr Winterbottom could have been involved and Boot took the Tewkesbury Abbey picture as some sort of backhander or bribe. I can see some merit in that and propose we interview the good doctor in the very near future. However, he can't be our murderer because he's far too old and frail to have overpowered William or strangled Mrs Boot.

'Neither do I buy William Boot's story about Alfred Latham selling the lot off without his son's knowledge, but at present we have no idea how anyone could have gained access to Latham Hall to carry out the deception. As well as the time needed to copy the paintings, there is the switching to be considered. Paintings are sizable objects; they can't be slipped into a pocket. Whoever did this not only must have been able to come and go as they pleased, but must have been able to carry the pictures about without arousing suspicion.'

'Sir, are we now working on the assumption that the Latham Hall paintings are the key to the murders and that the Dukoys, or this farmer, Simon Purslow, have nothing to do with it?' Aaron asked.

'We've investigating every possible lead, as we always do. But as it would seem a painting by this Alma chap that was once in the Latham collection has now disappeared from the home of two of our murder victims my instinct tells me this is the direction we should look in. The Dukoy development bears out what Masie Hintlesham and Quentin Makepeace said about the mayor being corrupt, and if nothing else tells us that he had no aversion to getting involved in something illegal if there was money in it for him, but however we look at it, I can't fit William Boot's death into the picture, and anyway, the Dellingbury deal was several years ago. Why would our killer wait so long if everyone knew at the time that Jonathan Boot was corrupt?' Having finished making his points, the DI turned to issue instructions to some of the team. 'Rose, can you find out where Winterbottom lives and make an appointment for us to see him ASAP.

'Ian, have you had a chance to look at William Boot's computer yet?'

'I've only had the time to give it a quick once-over, and there is precious little on it at all. Whatever he did in his working life, using a computer didn't seem to feature heavily, and if it's evidence the suicide note was written on it we're after then I've drawn a blank in the saved files. The next thing I'll need to do is deconstruct the hard drive to see what that contains, because that's where you find traces of everything — deleted files, unsaved files — but that will take me some time.' He was almost apologetic, knowing how urgently this information was wanted.

Mention of the suicide note made Cobb realize he hadn't informed his team of Dr Bolton's findings from yesterday's PM. 'It would appear Boot's hands were tied together before he was hanged. That means we are definitely looking at a third murder. I still want his computer gone through thoroughly. That so-called suicide note had to be typed on something. I know we're all busy but I would like you to do it tomorrow if you can, Ian. Before we call it a day, does anyone else have any ideas or thoughts they want to share?'

Perched on the edge of a desk, Bould shifted his weight slightly. 'I don't know whether this is of any significance, but Quentin Makepeace once said something that was rather strange.' He proceeded to outline his concern.

When he'd finished, Cobb became thoughtful. 'It could mean nothing, but you did right to mention it. Aaron, this is one for you to check out. Make it your priority. Leave Adam Boot for the time being. Start on this first thing in the morning.'

25

It wasn't the day for a long trip in a car, not with the sun beating down mercilessly from a cloudless sky. But at least they had a clear run on the M4, and Winterbottom lived on the right side of London for them, a fact Bould was profoundly thankful for as his boss wasn't known for patience when stuck in traffic jams. Just to the south of Kew Bridge, Bould swung the car round Kew Green before turning into Bushwood Road where he parked up.

'I thought you said there was no money in fine art,' Cobb grumbled, looking around at the expensive cars lining the very chi-chi street running parallel to the Thames.

'Winterbottom's an old man. He's probably lived here since before it was fashionable,' Bould said, rational as ever.

His boss grunted in disbelief, but refrained from replying.

They approached the front door, painted a vibrant pillar-box red, and almost before Bould's finger was off the bell the door was flung open.

'Come in, come in. I've been expecting

you,' their host said, sounding delighted to see them.

He led them into a commodious room at the back of the house, which surprised them by its modernity. The sanded board floors, littered with rugs in jewel-bright colours, the pale cream walls hung with hundreds of pictures, many of which were abstracts, the contemporary furniture, all surprised the officers who had expected to find something more traditional, more in keeping with an elderly academic bachelor.

'I'm sure you'd welcome some refreshments after your journey, so please make yourselves at home whilst I go and put the kettle on. Will Orange Pekoe be all right with you?'

'Let me do it, sir,' Bould said, having noticed once again how unsteady the old man was on his feet.

'Thank you for offering, Sergeant, but I can manage. I live here alone and cope surprisingly well. My niece calls in twice a week and does all my heavy shopping for me but I'm not ready for the care home just yet.'

It was impossible to tell from the way he spoke if he took exception to Bould's offer.

They waited whilst he pottered around in the kitchen, the occasional clunk of crockery or the tinkle of spoons reassuring them that he was as good as his word.

'Nice paintings,' Bould observed, wandering around the room and taking in the artwork.

'Abstracts are not my idea of a proper painting,' Cobb grumbled. 'Can't make head or tail of them. What's this supposed to be?' He looked in bemusement at a canvas that was nearly blank apart from a vivid green diagonal splashed messily across it. 'I suppose you're going to tell me this is worth thousands.'

'You don't think it lifts the room?' A dry chuckle from behind caused the DI to swing round. He hadn't heard the old man return. 'I've made some tea for us all, but it needs to brew a bit first.'

'I'm more your traditional sort. I prefer a painting of something I can recognize — like this.' Like a magician producing a rabbit from a hat, Cobb produced the enlarged copy of William's photograph with a flourish.

'Let me see.' Winterbottom produced a pair of pince-nez from his pocket, balanced them on the bridge of his nose and carefully studied the painting. 'Oh, now this is interesting. It's an Alma-Tadema without any doubt.'

'But it's not his usual subject matter,' Bould objected.

'No. This was a background study for his 1857 painting 'Faust and Marguerite'. In the finished piece, Faust and Marguerite are standing outside an abbey-type building, and this was intended to be nothing more than a preliminary study — and it used to be in the Latham collection.' He gave Cobb a shrewd look. 'All the artwork from there disappeared a long time ago. Do I take it you've found the originals?'

Cobb answered the question with one of his own. 'What would this painting be worth today if it was the genuine article?'

'Hundreds of thousands of pounds at the very least; possibly millions.' Winterbottom seemed surprised that the question needed to be asked.

'And do you recognize the man in the photograph?'

'I should think I do. It's my star pupil, Jonathan Boot. I would never forget him. Such a pity he never did his PhD. He would have gone on to great things, you know.'

'We think he probably did, but none of them were legal,' Cobb muttered, re-pocketing the picture. Now he had two positive IDs connecting Boot and the painting. 'Dr Winterbottom, can you think of any way in which Mr Boot could have gained possession of this painting, or access to the Latham collection?'

Shaking his head dolefully, Winterbottom said: 'I can't. I'm as amazed as I presume you are over this.'

'We know the collection was valued for insurance purposes in 1960, but that date doesn't allow us to place Mr Boot at the scene because he would have been far too young. Can you think of any circumstances that might have allowed him access to Latham Hall?'

'Well, now, let me go and pour the tea whilst I think about this.' Winterbottom shuffled off to the kitchen.

He returned a few minutes later, carrying a tray containing delicate cups of steaming dark brown tea and a plate of chocolate biscuits. Cobb's liking for the man increased.

'Help yourself,' Winterbottom invited. 'I'm not sure where Jonathan could fit into this, but something has come to mind. In July 1978 I was asked by Alfred Latham if I knew of anyone suitably qualified to go through all the family papers and catalogue the collection properly — that's a very different matter to an insurance valuation. I asked around and one of my colleagues, Dr Miriam Button, recommended Dr Timothy Townsend. He was considered extremely competent and able by Dr Button, and in need of employment. I passed on his name and contact details but I have no idea if he took the job.'

Cobb sipped his tea as Bould wrote down all the details, thoughtfully leaving a biscuit for his hard-working sergeant.

★ ★ ★

'I'll drive.' The DI stopped his sergeant as he was about to get into the driving seat.

It was an unusual occurrence, but Bould said nothing, guessing there was a reason that would soon be made clear to him. Handing the keys over, he went round to the front passenger seat and settled himself in.

'Does your phone have an internet connection?' Cobb asked.

When Bould confirmed it did, Cobb went on: 'Do a search for this Dr Timothy Townsend; if he's anywhere nearby we'll call in before we go home. July 1978 is the very time Boot disappeared from the scene.'

The car was like a furnace, so Cobb switched on the engine to get the air con up and running but he left the car out of gear until Bould had got the requested information. There was no point setting off until they knew where they were going.

It didn't take long. The internet was a wonderful thing, Cobb thought, although he and computers hadn't seen eye to eye in the beginning.

Bould was staring at the text on his screen as if it couldn't be right. 'Dr Timothy Townsend was killed in a car crash on 30 July 1978 in Surrey.'

'Are you sure that's the right man?'

'I've found several entries relating to him. He was only thirty-six when he died, but was a good painter in his own right. I've never heard of him but there are images of his work online and a potted biography. I think it must be the same man. One of them says he had a sister who had just graduated from St Martin's School of Art and was a promising painter, but after her brother's death she faded from the scene. No one knows what happened to her. The suggestion here is that she was so traumatized by her brother's accident that she became reclusive. Now the next bit might be a coincidence but her first name was Sylvia. Sylvia Townsend.'

26

The schools might have broken up but in London it didn't make a ha'porth worth of difference to the traffic. As Cobb fought his way on to Kew Bridge he had plenty of time to consider the information his sergeant had just given him.

Once he had the next steps clear in his mind, he issued further instructions. 'We can check this out easily enough. Ring Rose, or whoever's in the office, tell them to check Sylvia Boot's death certificate for her maiden name. I'm mindful of the fact that Mrs Boot told us she met her husband in London when they were both students. I'm always deeply suspicious of coincidences, and this one is looking increasingly unlikely. Whilst Rose is doing that I want you to ring Ms Warrinder at Latham Hall. See if any cataloguing work was done in 1978, and if so, by whom. Tell her to ring you back as soon as she's laid her hands on anything. If she rings before we're past Cirencester we'll stop off on the way back to the station.'

The call to Rose was brief, that to Jilly Warrinder somewhat longer, as she seemed to want to argue the toss. Cobb listened to half the conversation, hearing Bould become more and more exasperated.

'Yes, I know it was long before your time, but I'm assuming the family papers must be held somewhere, if not at the hall then at the county archives . . . This is extremely important . . . May I remind you we are conducting a murder enquiry . . . I know you are only the office manager but I would have thought this was exactly the sort of thing you would be expected to do and there isn't anyone else there to ask . . . I know the collection has disappeared and that's why it's important to know if the cataloguing went ahead . . . Ms Warrinder, I'm not asking you to do this, I'm telling you . . . Yes, thank you. You need to drop everything else and do this straightaway, and please ring me back when you've got the information . . . No, I want to know if the cataloguing was done and if it was, by whom and where the papers are. If you can get your hands on them immediately so much the better . . . Yes, thank you. Goodbye.' His sigh on ending the call was eloquence itself.

'You probably spoilt her day by giving her something to do. Until they replace Boot she must be having an easy time of it.'

'I think she feels it's beneath her, seeing as

how she's a qualified archaeologist.' It wasn't like Bould to be sarcastic, which showed how much she had riled him.

'We'll call in at Latham Hall regardless. If necessary we'll give her a not so gentle shove to get her going.'

But much to their surprise, before they reached their turnoff at Swindon, she called back to say she had what they wanted ready for them.

'So she's one of those who just like to make a fuss about things; probably thinks it makes her look more efficient when she actually does do as she's asked.' Cobb was wise in his understanding. Hadn't he worked with enough people like that in his time? Strangely, it was the ones who made the biggest song and dance who were the quickest and most effective at getting things done. It still didn't stop them being the most tiresome though.

The road from Swindon to Cirencester was a good one and they made excellent progress, but after they had turned off the A41 the road became single carriageway and they found themselves caught up in a long line of traffic crawling along behind a tractor.

'At this rate we won't get there before she goes home for the night,' Cobb said. He was never very good when stuck in traffic.

'Would you like me to take over the driving, sir?' Bould enquired in his best diplomatic voice.

'We won't get there any quicker.'

After that they proceeded in silence, until the tractor swung right into a field without any warning, nearly causing the car immediately behind to crash into it, but as the traffic speeded up, now this impediment to their progress was removed, Cobb brightened up considerably. He was only worried she'd have packed up for the day before they got there and he had a feeling that, at last, they were making headway with the investigation.

They arrived at Latham Hall at ten past three. The gardens were still closed to the public as they were being treated as a crime scene, so the car park was all but empty. Cobb drew up outside the little ticket booth, which was as near to the entrance as he could get. The booth was closed but the wooden gate into the gardens was ajar. There was no sign of any staff in the gardens or the schools centre, but the door leading into the main house was wide open and they walked through.

Having no idea where Jilly Warrinder's office was, Cobb called out: 'Ms Warrinder.' His voice echoed down the corridor and a door at the far end opened and Jilly stepped out.

'There wasn't enough room in my office for the files so I've put them in the ballroom. Come through and I'll show you what I've found.'

They followed her into a cavernous room. It must have been a splendid sight once. Remnants of an intricately moulded plaster ceiling defied gravity, clinging on in parts, although the floor was littered with grey, rotting chunks that had lost the battle. A magnificent marble fireplace filled half the length of one wall. The rest of the wall space contained wooden panels painted with a variety of bucolic scenes. The sole item of furniture was a large circular table, the edge of which was covered in dense, intricate carvings, and which stood in the middle of the room. On it rested a number of box files.

'The papers you want are in there.' She indicated the boxes. 'Sorry the light's not very good. The electrics aren't working in here as they've been deemed unsafe, so if you can't see well enough you'll have to go over to the window.'

'Thank you, Ms Warrinder. I'm impressed with the speed you got these for us,' Cobb responded gallantly.

'Actually, it wasn't difficult at all.' She was surprisingly chatty and friendly, and favoured them with a dazzling smile that transformed her face from nondescript to puckish. 'We've been using the attics as storerooms, so I'd been up there a few times and I'd seen that the Lathams had a whole lot of cupboards and cabinets up there with their family papers in them. There's a huge amount going back a couple of centuries. They seem to have been very conscious of their standing in society and kept every scrap of paper that related to their doings, but luckily they also filed them methodically and in chronological order. Everything has been fully dated as well. I suppose that shows how important they saw themselves as being. As all the cabinets and cupboards were clearly labelled with dates, it was quite simple to find the right month and year and then, look — ' She held up one of the boxes, turning it round so they could read the black lettering on the spine. 'See, whoever did this has marked it up properly. All these papers relate to the cataloguing and this box is dated August/September 1978, as is this.' She replaced the box and touched the next one in line. 'The third one is dated October 1978. I don't know if this is everything, but it's all there was up there.'

Bould flicked open the lid of the first box and took out a handful of papers. They were a mixture of sizes; some were handwritten, some were typed. Some were on lined paper, some on unlined. He shuffled them through his hands. He found something of interest. 'Look at this, sir.' He handed a sheet to his superior.

It was a handwritten letter to Alfred Latham and it was signed Timothy Townsend and dated 12 August 1978.

Cobb took in the significance. 'Ms Warrinder, we're going to have to take these three boxes with us. My sergeant will give you a receipt for them.'

She shrugged her shoulders in a way that was meant to convey it was all the same to her. 'Fine by me. Shouldn't think these papers are worth anything anyway as the art collection turned out to be forged.'

'On the contrary, Ms Warrinder. I can assure you these papers are worth their weight in gold,' Cobb said.

On the way back to the car, as Bould struggled to keep hold of the three overflowing boxes, Cobb said: 'We'll get a handwriting expert to compare that letter with a sample of Jonathan Boot's writing and if they match, as I very much hope they do, we've solved half this case. The trouble is it's not the right half.'

27

Apart from Aaron, the CID room was deserted. He was hunched over his computer, typing with a fierce concentration when Cobb and Bould returned. 'Rose has had to go to Molly's Gowns,' he said, then offered an explanation in response to Cobb's silent enquiry. 'It's a dress shop in Market Street. They've had some stock stolen. It looks like an inside job. But she asked me to tell you she's checked Mrs Boot's death certificate and her maiden name was — ' He broke off to consult the piece of paper with Rose's handwritten scrawl. 'Townsend.'

Cobb glanced at his sergeant. 'Looks like we've solved the mystery of how Boot got access to Latham Hall. Get those files put in the evidence room and then your next task is to get a sample of Boot's handwriting for comparison with a letter written by a dead man.'

'Sir?' Aaron looked up, intrigued.

'When Rose and Ian get back, I'll explain what we've found out. Where is Ian anyway?' Cobb looked round the room, only just registering the absence of his IT expert.

'He's gone to do something with the hard drive off William Boot's computer.'

Having looked at the time, Cobb changed his mind. 'We'll leave the debriefing until the morning then. Nine o'clock. Did you manage to dig out the info I asked you for yesterday?'

Aaron hit save, slid the keyboard away from him, and leant back in his chair. 'Still waiting for it to come through. I did ask first thing this morning, but they said it would take at least twenty-four hours, possibly longer depending on how many years they have to trawl through, so maybe tomorrow if we're lucky.'

Cobb blew out his cheeks. With the end of the case in sight he felt like a tethered dog being taunted by a big fat rabbit just out of his reach. 'Let's hope tomorrow it is then.'

Aware of his superior's frustration, Aaron threw out a bone. 'Still, that gave me time to continue looking into Adam Boot.'

'And?'

'Nothing, sir. He has cast-iron alibis for both his father's and his uncle's death, and his company seems to be thriving.'

'So we can at least eliminate one person from our list of suspects. That's something.' Cobb had the good grace to accept the bone for what it was worth. 'Not that it ever seemed really likely that Adam was our man.'

Later, having written up the day's case notes, the DI drove home knowing he wouldn't be able to relax until the final piece in the puzzle was resolved, and that wouldn't be until the following day at best. He needed a distraction and Sarah needed a treat. A quick detour off the main road and round into Orchard Street brought him to La Gondola Italian restaurant. He was able to bag a space right outside its door as a sleek Jaguar pulled out just as his rather more modest, and infinitely older, Toyota approached.

Mario, the canny owner whose real name was George, was visible through the plate glass chatting to his early-evening diners. La Gondola was a very popular place and it wouldn't normally be possible to reserve a table for the same evening at this late hour, but Mario owed him a few favours, which is why he had turned up in person.

When Mario saw the DI, he beamed in recognition and shot over.

'Meester Cobb, how wonderful eet iz to see you!' he cried, flinging his arms open wide.

Cobb grinned. 'Cut it out, George. I know you've never been nearer to Italy than the Roman remains at Bath.'

'Okey dokey. What can I do for you? No, actually before you tell me and spoil everything, come and have a drink on me.'

Cobb followed George through the dim and wonderfully cool interior to the bar and watched him pour two beers into tall cold glasses. The anticipation was almost as good as the beer would be.

'Cheers.' Cobb took his drink and the two formally clinked their glasses in salute before taking a deep draught. 'That's good, that's just what I needed. Now, George, any chance of a table for two for tonight?'

'A-ha! So at last you are going to treat your long-suffering wife to a night out. That poor woman, what she has to put up with. Where were you on Valentine's Day? I had a table reserved and what did you do — you cancelled at the last minute, that's what you did.'

'Yes, it was unfortunate but someone had the nerve to ruin my evening by robbing a petrol station that night. Try as I might, I just can't seem to get these villains to consider my home life. That's why I'm going to make it up to Sarah tonight, with your help.'

George rolled his eyes and put on his 'heaven help me' look. 'Valentine's Day was in February. It's now nearly August. Has it taken you six months to catch your petrol station thief? No, it hasn't!' A large hard-backed book was picked up, and a great show made of scanning through that evening's bookings. 'Looks like your lucky break has finally come, Mr Cobb. Be here at 9.30 sharp and I'll squeeze you in somehow.'

'Thanks, George.'

The owner gave a wolfish grin, showing two rows of unnaturally white and even teeth. 'I wouldn't thank me until you see the bill.'

28

A nailable lie. That's all he ever looked for. And here it was.

The information had come through at lunchtime the next day and Cobb had immediately called the whole team together. As this could well be the end to their hunt for the person who had killed three members of the same family, he felt it only right they should all hear the news at once.

Aaron leant back in his chair, looking pleased with himself as he assessed the impact his discovery had on the team.

'Arrange for a search warrant ASAP,' Cobb said. 'If we find what I think we'll find, we've got our killer.'

Just over two hours later, they were standing on the doorstep of 48 Poppyfield Crescent waiting for Quentin Makepeace to answer the bell.

'Good morning, Inspector, Sergeant,' Makepeace began politely enough on seeing them. 'What can I — '

Cobb cut him short. 'We've a warrant here to search your house.' He produced the document.

'What on earth?' Makepeace remained firmly blocking the doorway, and although he managed to sound innocently baffled a look of panic had briefly flared in his eyes. He recovered quickly. 'What are you expecting to find?'

'We'll tell you when we find it,' the DI said, and shouldered his way past Makepeace.

It was upstairs in the bedroom, on the wall above his bed.

'Sergeant.' Cobb nodded to Bould, who took down the painting and bagged it. Then Cobb turned to Makepeace, who was staring out of the window as if he was no longer part of the proceedings. 'Quentin Makepeace, I am arresting you for the murders of Jonathan, William and Sylvia Boot.'

Makepeace didn't seem to hear. 'That painting is rightfully mine, you know,' he said mildly. 'I want it back when you've finished with it.'

'Yes, I know it's yours. Is that why you killed them, just to get a picture back?'

'Good Lord, no.' The man appeared genuinely shocked. 'I killed them because they drove my father to suicide, my mother to an early grave and ruined my future. How did you find out who I was?'

'You know, if you're going to lie it's best to try to keep it within an area you know something about. If you'd told us the truth about working in India you could have talked about the country with some authority and we might never have had any reason to doubt you. Instead you claimed you'd worked in the Serengeti National Park in Kenya. Unfortunately for you, my sergeant here is an educated man and he knew that the Serengeti Park is entirely in Tanzania. I had quite a geography lesson from him on the subject, and he told me that the northern boundary of the Serengeti Park is the Mara River, and on the other side is the Masai Mara Game Reserve — now that's in Kenya. Apparently it's still part of the Serengeti *plain* but not the *park.* What made you lie to us in this way? Why did you say you'd been in Africa?'

'Because I didn't want you to find out who I was,' Makepeace said patiently, as if explaining to an idiot. 'I thought I'd covered my traces pretty well but I couldn't be sure you wouldn't go checking up on me so I thought it best not to mention India — doctors are always easy to trace because they have to be registered.'

'And so you told us you'd been a missionary,' Cobb said, sounding almost admiring. 'That had us fooled for a time. Harmless sort of fellows is how we think of missionaries, not the type likely to go around killing people, not when they are supposed to be full of Christian love and compassion. Mark you, the same should be said of doctors. Of course, once we suspected you had lied to us about Africa, we asked ourselves, now why would he do that? Perhaps he isn't all he appears to be. And then we asked ourselves, what about the missing Latham son — where did he go? All we knew was that he'd been a doctor in London, but the great thing about doctors, as you've already told us, is that they have to be registered, and that means it isn't difficult to find out where they are working — or in your case, where they had been working. Perhaps you should have changed your name a long time ago.'

'Perhaps I should.' After this curt reply, a silence developed, broken only by the loud ticking of an old-fashioned clock in a walnut casing on the old-fashioned tiled mantelpiece.

Looking round the room there was a sense of time having stood still. The bedroom with its small tiled fireplace was unchanged from the 1930s, and the iron-framed bed also seemed to date from that period. Makepeace had only bought the house some eighteen months earlier and yet he had stamped nothing of his personality on it. It was just a shelter for him, somewhere to sleep and eat, something entirely impersonal — if it hadn't been for the painting of Tewkesbury Abbey that had hung above the bed.

Cobb could afford to wait until his quarry chose to break the silence. Sooner or later he would; they always did. The need to confess seemed to be a human compunction.

And eventually the time came. 'Do you want to know why I joined the International Red Cross and went abroad? It was because I wanted to help other people — I mean really help others. People whose lives are so grim and poverty stricken that no one in this country can even begin to imagine what it's like; children dying from diseases that have long been eradicated in the West. I wanted to do what I could to ease the suffering of others. It helped me to know that something good came out of the suffering Boot and his wife inflicted upon my family, so I suppose in a funny sort of way I should be grateful to them because I would never have thought of going otherwise. For years I'd been working in a hospital in London and I was ticking along nicely. I would have made consultant in due course, but then my grandfather died and you know the rest.'

'Most of it,' Cobb admitted. 'We know your grandfather wanted the collection cataloguing properly and the man who was going to do it

304

was killed in a car crash.'

'It was my grandfather's great misfortune that Townsend's sister had just married Jonathan Boot. He was a mature graduate in fine art and was around the same age as Townsend. My grandfather had never met either man, so Boot must have realized how easy it would be to pass himself off as Dr Townsend. He was also a damn good painter, I'll give the devil that.'

'The forgery didn't come to light until 1984,' Bould pointed out. 'How did you know Boot was responsible?'

'I didn't know it was him to begin with. I thought it was Timothy Townsend because when the collection was valued in 1960 there was no doubt that the paintings were the originals, and Townsend was the only person who had the opportunity between then and my grandfather's death to carry out this crime.'

Those points cleared up, Cobb was anxious to move on. 'How did you find out that Timothy Townsend was really Jonathon Boot?'

'When I retired and came back to Mallerton I decided to look for Townsend. Those years in India hadn't stopped me brooding over what had happened. I thought they would; I *hoped* they would. I don't

305

consider myself a bitter or vindictive person but it seemed only proper and just that Townsend should answer for his crime.' He paused and looked at the officers for confirmation that he had done the right thing. He didn't get it. 'So I set out to find him, only to discover Townsend had been killed in a car crash before he ever got to Latham Hall. But somebody had turned up and carried out his work.

'Do you find the internet useful, Inspector? I do. I don't know how we managed without it. It only took a matter of minutes for me to find out all I needed to know about Townsend and that he had a sister who also was a painter and her name was Sylvia. I wasted a lot of time trying to track her down without any joy, until I had a brainwave. What if she had got married? Well, she'd have a different name so then it was just a matter of getting a copy of her marriage certificate and tracking her down, and that was much easier than I thought it would be because I stumbled across her and that devil she married quite by chance.'

'It must have been quite a shock to find them still here in Mallerton,' Bould observed.

A shadow crossed the doctor's face. His fists balled as he thought of all those years they had lived with impunity in the shadow of his former home. 'It certainly was. Perhaps I should start at the beginning so you can understand the order of things. Believe it or not, it's important to me that you fully appreciate just what has been going on here in Mallerton.

'About eighteen months ago, I retired. Unsure as to where I wanted to live I came home to England to see how I would settle. Many ex-pats find it very difficult, you know, and I didn't want to make that sort of mistake. I rather like India, and after over twenty years away, well, Britain has changed and I didn't know if I would be able to adjust. I stayed in a hotel in Bournemouth — having been hundreds of miles from the sea for so many years I had a hankering to live on the coast, and with Latham Hall long sold there was certainly nothing to bring me back to Mallerton except for bitter memories.

'That was when I decided to track down Townsend. I honestly don't know what I was going to do, just confront him, I think, make him apologize for what he did to me and my family. Imagine my surprise when I discovered he had died *before* he catalogued our collection. I don't know about the police, Inspector, but in all my years' experience as a doctor I have found it the case that dead men are incapable of doing anything at all, so I asked myself who had passed themselves off as Dr Townsend and gained entry to Latham Hall, because that person was without any doubt at all in my mind the person responsible for stealing my inheritance. After I had acquired Sylvia Townsend's marriage certificate I decided Jonathan Boot was the man responsible but I had no idea where he was.'

He stopped again and laughed. 'Life's full of coincidences, have you noticed?' That this was a rhetorical question was apparent because he hurried on without pause. 'The coincidence in this case being that shortly after I arrived in England a cousin of mine from Mallerton died and I came over for the funeral, and there *he* was on the front page of the local paper. The leader of Mallerton District Council claiming credit for securing ten million pounds from the National Lottery to restore Latham Hall gardens to their full glory. There was a picture of the bastard smiling as he stood on the terrace of my house! If he'd walked into the room there and then I'd have killed him with my bare hands. Instead, I went back to Bournemouth, paid my hotel bill off and came back to Mallerton as Quentin Makepeace. Boot had never met me so he had no idea who I was.'

'Why wait over a year to kill him?' Bould

asked, scribbling frantically.

'Well, now, you see. Once I started to consider my plans I realized I could make him suffer. There was no hurry. I'd waited over twenty years as it was. A few more wouldn't hurt. I went to every council meeting and always found some way to needle him. It got to him no end; probably more than the anonymous letters I sent to him and his wife. You might think this was very petty and trivial, but I gained a certain pleasure out of it — not least because I knew he had no idea who I really was. And I wasn't after money. Money wouldn't bring my father back, or my mother who died a broken woman only two years after my father. I wanted to frighten the pair of them. She was involved too, you know. They worked as a pair and through the people they knew in the art world they had the contacts to sell them on. A nice start to married life, wouldn't you say — to have the best part of a million pounds in the bank? I doubt they ever lost any sleep over my father's death, so I thought I should redress the balance. After I saw that newspaper item I knew I would kill them but I wanted to unnerve them first. I wanted them to feel they had to always look over their shoulder, to sleep with one eye open, and then, one day — ' He snapped his fingers. 'I chose atropine because

I knew his death would be humiliating. It causes hysteria and hallucinations, and is rare enough for no one to work out what it was in time to administer the antidote, even if they had it to hand which I doubt very much they would.'

'Where did you get it from?' Bould asked.

'I used to be a doctor,' Makepeace said, as if this was news to them. 'Luckily if kept in the right conditions it has a shelf life of between two and five years.

'Until Boot's death I don't think his wife took my threats seriously, but for the last few days of her life — well, you saw her. She was a nervous wreck.' Satisfaction at the memory cut his narrative short. Hands in pockets, Makepeace smirked at the officers. He was jaunty, well pleased with himself. Cobb thought it likely he'd get off with insanity.

Now he was talking, Makepeace seemed unable to stop. It was often the way. He wanted them to know just how very clever he had been. He started to strut around the room. 'I did hope to be able to poison that bitch as well, but I didn't have the opportunity. Not surprising really. She'd have been on her guard for poison. I didn't enjoy strangling her. It was most unpleasant.'

'I expect Mrs Boot would have said the same.' Cobb's voice had a hard edge to it and

Makepeace acknowledged the irony with a wry smile. 'How did you administer the poison to Mr Boot?'

'I'd been waiting for the opportunity for a long time, but I knew that if I bided my time, one day I'd be able to do it. That was the one good thing about him being mayor. He had to attend a lot of civic functions that were open to the public, so I could be there, dogging his footsteps. He thought it was because I'm some sort of nutter with nothing better to do with my time than check up to see if our elected leaders are not abusing their expenses but he couldn't have been further from the truth.

'On the day in question he was opening a community centre. He was the only council-lor there, and the head of whatever it was from the council had never met me so no one else recognized me. The mayor made a speech, cut the ribbon and then everyone had a cup of tea and a piece of cake.

'Atropine is widely used by doctors and I've still got some medical supplies. It was the ideal thing. I needed the contents of several phials because you do need a big dose to kill someone. So I decanted them into a bottle small enough to slip into my pocket. Then, when he was being shown around the display of paintings done by the nursery group who

311

were going to be using the new centre, how easy it was to slip the poison into his tea. You might think it would be difficult but it wasn't.

'All you have to do is distract someone. Magicians call it misdirection. I deliberately bumped into the person standing behind the mayor, and that pushed her into Boot. He turns round, they are both busy apologizing to each other, and I put the atropine into his tea and nobody notices. Clever, don't you think?' His expression suddenly changed from smugness to annoyance. He'd noticed a pair of his shoes beside the chest of drawers weren't lined up with each other. He rushed across the room, got down on his hands and knees and carefully moved the left shoe an inch or so, until it lay straight against the right.

Remaining on the floor, he rocked back on his heels and looked up at Cobb, his equanimity restored. 'It only took a second to do.' He grinned at Cobb, who stared back impassively. Then Makepeace went on: 'As I said, I'd have liked to have poisoned his wife as well, but strangling her did have its advantages. I was able to let her know who I was before she died. That was satisfying. I felt as if the wheel had turned full circle.'

'And the son? Why did you send Adam threatening letters? You must have known he had no part in his parents' deception.'

Makepeace sprang to his feet, his face dark with rage. 'Deception? That's a nice word for what they did to my family. It was fraud of the most callous and calculating kind. They ruined our lives.' He was literally spitting with fury, dancing on the spot before realizing how out of control he must seem, because he cleared his throat, turned half away and took a deep breath before turning back to address the officers. 'I never intended to harm Adam because as you say, he had no part in any of this. Although Boot caused innocent people to suffer, I wasn't coming down to his level, but I thought by continuing with the letters you might be distracted into looking for a different motive. Misdirection again, you see, which is why I deliberately chose the wrong version of 'your'. Naturally, I didn't want to be caught.'

'No murderer ever does,' Bould said sardonically.

'What about William Boot?' asked his boss. 'Was he involved in the fraud?'

'Ah yes, William Boot. He was just as bad in his own way. He cashed in on my family's misfortune. It may have been a long time later, but it was still the same thing. Don't you see, Inspector, the whole diabolical Boot family made money out of ruining my family?' The passion he was feeling was undeniable.

'Did you know William had no part in stealing the artwork?' Cobb said.

'I didn't know one way or the other. But I did find out William had no right to the high position he held in my family home. Did you know Lathams had lived there since 1543? Not in the current house, of course — that's Georgian — but there was a fine Tudor mansion house on the site first. Over 400 years we'd been there and then overnight we were ruined by knaves and scoundrels.

'How did William Boot get that job? He had neither qualifications, knowledge or experience. It was another scam engineered by his brother. The three of them were rotten to the core. I would say I've done the world a favour by getting rid of them.' He folded his arms and looked defiant, daring the officers to disagree with him.

'How did you know Boot had the Alma-Tadema painting?' Bould asked.

'I didn't. Wasn't I lucky in finding it? One tiny part of my inheritance back where it belongs.' Makepeace stopped his narrative to savour the moment. He was still smiling when he took up his story again. 'After I killed Sylvia I decided to have a look round their house just out of curiosity. The French windows were open; I didn't break in.'

How virtuous he sounded. As if breaking and entering was a much more serious crime than murder. He seemed to think he had done nothing wrong — nothing wrong at all.

★   ★   ★

It was well into the evening. Makepeace had been charged and was languishing in the cells below ready for his appearance before the magistrates in the morning, but there was no chance of an early night for Cobb, as he had to review all the cases that had taken a back seat whilst the team dealt with the Boot murders.

Still, it wasn't all bad news. Because he wouldn't be home until late he'd eaten in the staff canteen and had a good dinner of steak and kidney pie and chips followed by apple crumble drowned in custard. It beat steamed haddock and broccoli any day.

We do hope that you have enjoyed reading this large print book.

Did you know that all of our titles are available for purchase?

We publish a wide range of high quality large print books including:
Romances, Mysteries, Classics
General Fiction
Non Fiction and Westerns

Special interest titles available in large print are:
The Little Oxford Dictionary
Music Book
Song Book
Hymn Book
Service Book

Also available from us courtesy of Oxford University Press:
Young Readers' Dictionary
(large print edition)
Young Readers' Thesaurus
(large print edition)

For further information or a free brochure, please contact us at:
Ulverscroft Large Print Books Ltd.,
The Green, Bradgate Road, Anstey,
Leicester, LE7 7FU, England.
Tel: (00 44) **0116 236 4325**
Fax: (00 44) **0116 234 0205**

DEAD IN THE WATER

Veronyca Bates

Can we escape our past misdeeds? It seems not, as Eliza Hobbis' past catches up with her in a deadly way . . . When Eliza's body is fished out of Cotton Park gravel pits, the police believe it's suicide, but it quickly becomes apparent Eliza was murdered. If she had something to hide it was too well hidden for the police — there's no suspect or motive to assist them. As another body is found in the same gravel pits, the police are uncertain whether they are looking for one killer or two. DI Cobb faces his most baffling case . . .

TOMB OF THE SERPENT

Guy Fraser

Superintendent Henry Jarrett thinks he has encountered murder in all its forms, but gory human sacrifice is horribly new. Is there a madman loose in Victorian Glasgow, as Jarrett, Inspector Grant and Sergeant Quinn believe? The victims are randomly chosen, the killings unpredictable and thus unsolvable. Then, a murder at a travelling fair — which bears no resemblance to the others — and the little matter of the valuable artefacts, increases Jarrett's confusion. It seems the time is right for him to tie the knot with his beloved Elsie Maitland and retire to the seaside — before his chief constable demands his resignation.

ROCK TO DEATH

John Paxton Sheriff

In Gibraltar, Jack Scott finds a corpse —
after seeing Nick Skaill walking out of a
nightclub with a gun in his hand. But from
the moment he informs the police, his life
is in danger. Skaill's father is criminal
Ronnie Skaill, a Briton living in Spain,
who now wants to remove the only witness
to this crime. Meanwhile, Liverpool
detective Mike Haggard suspects Scott's
brother, Tim, of a double murder.
Bizarrely, the case suggests links to the
Skaills. As Scott struggles with the puzzle's
growing complications, there are more
murders _ followed by a bloody climax on
Gibraltar's rocky slopes.

A WATERY GRAVE

Jean Chapman

Out on a morning run, ex-Met officer John Cannon vaults a stile, becomes ensnared in a discarded fishing line — and entangled in trouble. For there is a macabre discovery at the far end of this line, leading John into a search for a missing au pair, which puts him into conflict with the local police and involvement with international crime. He discovers that the local Health Spa has much to conceal, with its security guards and dogs patrolling the grounds. But the Portuguese owner is a ruthless businessman, and Cannon faces danger every step of the way . . .

MERCENARY

Paul Bennett

When Johnny Silver's brother, Carlo, the head of an investment bank, disappears — along with ten million euros — Johnny, an ex-mercenary on the run, is persuaded to come out of hiding to track him down. The trail takes Johnny deep into the world of gambling, prostitution, drugs and human trafficking, leading to a crime that shocks the core of a man who had thought he had seen everything . . .

A NARROW EXIT

Faith Martin

Detective Inspector Hillary Greene is due to retire in a matter of weeks. But her boss, determined to get her to change her mind about leaving the force, gives her a murder inquiry to handle. The victim, Michael Ivers, a gambler and a notorious womaniser, had few friends and there's a long list of murder suspects. Hillary has just days to find out who killed him — or her final case will be an unsolved murder. To add to an already complicated case, her old foe, ex-Sergeant Frank Ross is back on the scene — and a prime suspect . . .